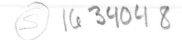

A Matter Of Pride
and Other Stories

by
Nicholasa Mohr

Arte Público Press
Houston, Texas
1997

This volume is made possible through grants from the National Endowment for the Arts (a federal agency), Andrew W. Mellon Foundation, the Lila Wallace-Reader's Digest Fund and the City of Houston through The Cultural Arts Council of Houston, Harris County.

Recovering the past, creating the future

Arte Público Press
University of Houston
Houston, Texas 77204-2090

Detail from the right panel of the
painting "Mirada," 1995 by José Morales ©
Cover design by Gladys Ramirez

Mohr, Nicholasa.
    A Matter of pride and other stories /
    by Nicholasa Mohr.
       p.   cm.
    ISBN 1-55885-163-1 (alk. paper).
    —ISBN 1-55885-177-1 (pbk.: alk. paper)
    1. Puerto Rican women—New York (State)—
New York—Fiction. 3. New York (N.Y.)—Fiction.
I. Title.
P83563.036M38   1997
813'. 54—dc21   96-39826
                                         CIP

A Matter Of Pride
and Other Stories

Also By Nicholasa Mohr

Rituals of Survival: A Woman's Portfolio
In Nueva York
El Bronx Remembered
Nilda
Felita
Going Home
The Magic Shell
Growing Up Inside the Sanctuary of My Imagination
The Song of El Coquí and other tales of Puerto Rico
Old Letivia and The Mountain of Sorrows

Place of Refuge

The water clock
strikes
and I remember
who I am.
At midnight,
at dawn,
at the edge
of darkest hours,
at the invisible
rim of time.

From the book *The Mirror is Always There* ©1992,
a collection of poems by Alba Ambert.

For Jay Elz and Alba Ambert, your being there has made a significant and wonderful difference.

I wish to thank The Helene Wurlitzer Foundation in Taos, New Mexico, for providing a quiet haven where I was able to complete the final revisions for this collection of stories.

Nicholasa Mohr

Contents

A Matter of Pride 9

In Another Place in a Different Era 42

My Newest Triumph 66

Memories: R.I.P. 84

Rosalina de los Rosarios 107

Blessed Divination 135

Utopia, and the Super Estrellas 169

A Matter of Pride

It was a sweltering afternoon in the city of Ponce, Puerto Rico, in August of 1959. I was twenty-one years old and a new bride who had been married one week earlier. Laying naked under the mosquito netting that was draped over the large four-poster bed, I listened to the low hum of the ceiling fan as it circulated the hot air. I reached toward the foot of the bed, lifted the elaborately hand-embroidered cotton bed cover that had been neatly folded and pulled it over my body. Slowly and mindfully I wiped off the sweat that had accumulated underneath my breasts, and on my stomach and crotch.

"God, this must be what living in hell feels like," I gasped.

I needed to go to the bathroom, but I was too hot and uncomfortable to get myself out of bed. I turned my head and saw that my nightgown was lying alongside the empty space beside me.

"What a stinking way to spend my honeymoon. Shit!"

My eyelids, heavy with perspiration, closed involuntarily as if sealed shut by the heat, and in a few moments I felt myself slipping into a deep sleep. I must have slept soundly because, when the droning of a tenacious mosquito woke me, my chin was covered with saliva and my throat felt like sandpaper. Over and over it circled overhead, then careened into the net attacking the area over my left shoulder. Patiently, I watched as the mosquito went into a frenzy eager to get a nip of my flesh. Carefully I pressed my shoulder against the transparent fabric and held perfectly still and waited. When I felt its sting I clutched a fistful of netting and tightened my grip until the buzzing dwindled. "Good!" I shouted, pretending I had just squeezed the life right out my brand-new husband, "Die, Charlie! Die *cabrón,* you mother fucking bastard." The bright blood and black specks smeared across my open palm gave me a feeling of power, and I giggled joyfully. I knew it was silly, but I took pleasure in this instant victory.

Outside, a dense veil of hot, humid air was draped over the city of Ponce, festering underneath the scorching noon sun. By midday, summer temperatures would often climb past 100 degrees Fahrenheit. On the second day of my arrival here, I had foolishly thought I'd take a walk before lunch. But the blinding sun and burning heat forced me off the streets along with the entire populace. Roads were free of people and traffic. Even stray dogs and cats sought refuge in the shade of the alleyways and back yards. Public offices and shopkeepers, the whole town, closed down for two hours. Midday was a time when folks went home, showered, ate an abundant *almuerzo* and then took their *siesta*. Air-conditioning barely existed in Puerto Rico in the late 1950's, and significant changes in the island's social customs had not yet taken place.

Three days after we arrived at his cousin's house in Ponce, my bridegroom announced that he was off to see an old friend. "I contacted some of the guys I knew when I was a kid in P.R... real good buddies of mine. Rudolfo Albániz was my ace. Man, he and me were real tight, and we ain't seen each other since we were teenagers. Rudolfo arranged for a few of us guys to get together for a little reunion in Humacao, over by the east coast. So..., Paula, it's only men. No girls allowed and no place for you. My old lady ain't gonna be the only piece of tail there with a bunch of horny machos. Understand? I might be back very late tonight, or even tomorrow. Just so you know."

Charlie had been gone since early Wednesday. Today was Friday and I didn't have a clue as to his actual whereabouts or when he would return.

Exactly one week before in the South Bronx, I had married Charles Eduardo Gómez. We exchanged vows in a simple ceremony at Saint Anselm's Roman Catholic Church. There were no bridesmaids, no ushers. Willie, Charlie's older brother, was best man, and Stella Puig, my close girlfriend, was my maid of honor. My own parents

were dead. My mother had died after a long bout
with breast cancer when I was sixteen. The following year, my dad died of complications during a her-
nia operation. He was older than my mother and
had two sons from a previous marriage. Besides my
parents, my half brothers were my only other relatives in the States. But I hardly ever saw them,
although the youngest of the two, Victor, did show
up at St. Anselm's and stayed for our small wedding
reception. I was so pleased to have at least one
member of my family attend. And I was so proud to
show off my older brother to everyone.

Charlie's people were unpretentious and hard-
working folks who never interfered in our lives or
had much to say about anything. Their one goal in
life was to save enough money to return to their
beloved Puerto Rico, buy a good piece of property
and build a large house. His mother, Eugenia, had
worked at the same large hotel in midtown Manhattan as assistant salad chef for eighteen years.
She had never gotten a promotion nor had she ever
been relieved from her early shift starting at 5 A.M.
But I never once heard her complain. She had
raised three sons and a daughter. Charlie was the
older middle child. On my wedding day, Eugenia
took me aside to say that all she wanted in this life
was to see her children happily married and to
enjoy her grandchildren. "Paula, *mi hijita*," she said
with tears in her eyes. "I wish the same for you."

Charlie and I had agreed that it would be sense-
less to use up our savings on a large wedding.

Instead, we would spend a generous part of our reserves on a meaningful honeymoon. "Something we could remember for the rest of our lives, baby," was how Charlie put it. The balance of our money would remain in the bank, earning interest. We had plans for our future, for sure.

Soon after, Charlie came up with the idea for a great honeymoon, a vacation that wouldn't cost too much money. "My cousin Roberto's always inviting us to stay with him and his family in Ponce. I told you, he's a veteran of the Korean War, went through college under the G.I. Bill and became a lawyer. His wife's a pharmacist, educated, and comes from a high-class family with plenty of bread. They live in a great house, terrific place. I shown you pictures, remember? Roberto and his old lady speak pretty good English, too. I say we rent a car and go stay with them for a while, then travel around the island."

I was born in the Bronx and, although I had never been to the island, my parents often spoke longingly about their homeland. Like Charlie's folks, they too had held the dream of returning home some day. They would refer to their region of Barranquitas, in the highlands of Puerto Rico, as *nuestro paraíso*. Growing up, I shared my parent's sense of displacement and loss. After they died, my sorrow was intensified by the reality of their unrequited dream, and I developed a longing to see Puerto Rico. I felt that on this trip I might somehow make it up to my parents by visiting their beloved homeland. I didn't need much convincing. Going to Puerto Rico seemed like a perfect idea.

Besides, I was accustomed to having Charlie dictate my life. We met when I was seventeen, right after my father died. I was still a virgin and had never seriously dated. Charlie was twenty-four and had a reputation of being wild and chasing women—a much admired *macho*. Soon after we began going steady, Charlie settled down.

People said I was good for him. As our relationship developed, Charlie assumed a paternal role. "Baby, it's only natural," he liked to tell me, "that I be the one to guide and protect you. I'll teach you what you need to know, Mami. You gotta listen, Paula, and do like I say, because I'm older and wiser, so I know what's good for you." As I got older, I began to disagree with Charlie, which resulted in quarrels, lots of quarrels. In fact, it seemed that with each passing year our arguing increased.

In those days, I worked as a receptionist in a major insurance firm. At night I had enrolled in City College, determined to get my degree in Business Administration. As for having children, that was somewhere in the distant future, "My college degree comes first." I was clear on that point and said so. "No way am I staying a file clerk or a receptionist forever, Charlie. I've got better plans for my life."

At school, one of my teachers recommended I read an anthology about women who helped to change American history. I read with awe about the lives of Sojourner Truth, Jane Addams, Margaret Sanger and other powerful women. I was amazed by these accounts of female independence. My newly acquired knowledge about the issue of women's rights and freedom provoked our worst disputes. Charlie dismissed my assertions and refused to acknowledge my views.

Once, I decided to share a section from *The Second Sex* by Simone De Beauvoir with Charlie and quoted from her chapter on "The Independent Woman": "It is through gainful employment that woman has traversed most of the distance that separated her from the male; and nothing else can guarantee her liberty in practice. Once she ceases to be a parasite, the system based on her dependence crumbles; between her and the universe there is no longer any need for a masculine mediator."

"You're reading crap again! What do you mean, that women should have the same rights like guys? Don't be comparing yourself to me because you still need what I got. Do you pee standing up, girl?"

I wasn't about to walk away from that argument so easily, especially when I had proof positive. "No," I shouted, holding up De Beauvoir's book, "... but I don't use what's between my legs for no meal ticket either. I work for what's mine and I do what I like! I'm a free agent and YOU don't fucking own me!"

And, so it went a good deal of the time.

Charlie was also a jealous man who repeatedly insisted that I not wear tight clothing or show cleavage. That was when I would tighten my belt an extra notch, or undo another button on my blouse. In spite of my Latina upbringing, I always found it difficult to conform to the demands of males who declare themselves to be in charge. This is probably because being passive was never part of my nature.

Whenever Charlie became too overbearing, I argued back and threatened to leave him. Once, I even packed up all of my things and went to stay with a friend. It took just a few hours until Charlie found me and begged me to come back, promising to alter his ways. "Come on, Paula, I like your spirit. Give me time to get used to some of your crazy ideas. Look, I don't want no dish rag for my old lady. You're smart and beautiful. I want my feisty baby. I can't live without my baby. I love you, Mami... don't hurt me like this. I love you!"

He knew just how to con me and keep me off balance, because, invariably, I believed him. In spite of all my lip service to feminism, I felt incapable of seriously challenging him. Charlie had become my substitute parent. He represented the stability I craved, and I preferred to overlook his jealous outbursts and his need to dominate me. I felt Charlie was all the family I had and his support mattered more than anything. When he praised me for being smart, approved of my going to school and agreed to postpone having a family, I responded with gratitude and loyalty.

Actually, he was motivated by personal ambition. "Now that I've got my baby trained just the way I want her," he often joked, "I don't want no kids spoiling things. And I gotta make sure Paula stays that way, too." I'd laugh along with everybody else. I cherished his concern for me and never saw a hidden agenda. If anyone had asked back then how I felt about Charlie, I would have told them that I couldn't imagine my life without him.

Charlie was a hard worker. He had been steadily employed for five years as an auto mechanic for General Motors in Tarrytown, New York, and was up for a promotion. Both of us had managed to accumulate an extra week with pay, in addition to regular vacation time. That meant three whole weeks off. We had it all neatly planned too. One week would be set aside so that we could paint and fix up our new apartment, but first, we would spend the other two weeks on a fabulous vacation and a romantic honeymoon. "One we would never forget," promised Charlie.

After we spent two nights at a moderately priced hotel right off the Condado, in San Juan, Charlie rented a car. He drove through the narrow country routes, past the mountainous regions and over La Piquiña, the treacherous winding roads near Cayey. Finally, after a good six hours of motoring almost non-stop across the island, we arrived in Ponce.

Roberto Francisco Gómez was of a medium height and a hefty build. With a boisterous greeting, he swaggered toward us and introduced his family: María Elena Gómez and their two children, Luz María, aged ten, and Robertito, aged eight. He had no qualms about bragging that he was a prominent attorney who was working his way toward being appointed a municipal court judge. María Elena, a petite woman, stood by shyly while her husband relayed all of their family's achievements. His wife worked at a large pharmacy where she was also the manager, and his children attended the most exclusive and expensive private Catholic school in Ponce. By next year, he assured us, we'd all have to address him as Judge Gomez.

Roberto then emphasized the importance of my visit in particular. "You were born here, Charlie, but your wife should know about her culture and learn what it means to be *una mujer puertorriqueña*. Here, we value tradition. Men are men and women are women, eh? Women are respected because they know their place. Here is NOT the American way. Here... IS the Puerto Rican way. Paula, you'll learn."

I wasn't pleased by his words and was just about to tell Roberto, when he abruptly changed gears. His voice took on a conciliatory voice. "But, *primita, tú y mi primo* will also have a wonderful time here in Ponce. And, María Elena, you'll take proper care of her, right?"

"Of course, I'll take excellent care of Paula. And, Charlie, you can rest assured that I'll personally keep a sharp eye on your bride."

Her words sounded even more intimidating than Roberto's. Was she planning to spy on me? Later, I told Charlie that this whole situation made me uneasy.

"What was all that shit Roberto was talking about? Here IS the Puerto Rican way? Who put him in charge? And, what's he mean, men are men, and women are women? Doesn't he know that already? For a lawyer he's not very bright!"

Charlie said that Roberto simply liked to hear himself talk. "That's why the dude wants to be a judge, so he can talk a whole lot of bullshit. Don't be taking him so seriously."

"*Coño*, Charlie, María Elena better not think I'm going to be hanging out with her. I'm here on my honeymoon, remember? I'm not here to play little girlfriend games with her. She talks like I'm a kid that she has to keep an eye on. What's all that *mierda* about? Because I don't like what's going down in this place, Charlie. Uh... uh, not at all!" I had a strong urge to pack up and leave right then and there, but I also didn't want to upset Charlie and start an argument on our first night.

"Take it easy, Paula. She's just a simple woman trying to be a good hostess. Anyway, once in a while you two girls could hang out... like if sometime I can go out with Roberto. That's how they do things here. Come on, you don't want to hurt their feelings, Mami. They're trying to be nice to us. You can handle it... you know you can. Baby, you're smart, very smart, right? Look, it's only for a few days. Ain't no big deal."

Reluctantly, I agreed that since it was only temporary, maybe it wasn't such a big deal. Actually, I had good reason to be apprehensive at the possibility of being separated from my new husband. From the outset of our relationship four years earlier, Charlie had made it clear that Friday nights out with the guys was his right.

"God-given," he had declared, *"y mi derecho, because I'm a man."*

Charlie ignored all of my protests, and in time I learned to accept Charlie's Friday nights out. At the beginning, when he would return late Saturday or early Sunday morning, I'd scream, weep and make threats. But as time passed, I mostly sulked and never truly dared challenge him. Although I hated his guts when he was gone, I was always relieved when he came home to me. Because when I asked myself, what would I do and where would I go if Charlie never came back, I had no answers.

But on our honeymoon I had expected it was going to be different. I just knew he wouldn't go off and leave me alone in a distant place with virtual strangers. I honestly believed he wouldn't dare.

During our first two days in Ponce, I had a nice enough time. Charlie and I drove out west to see the seaport city of Mayagüez, and we swam at the regional beaches. Charlie's relatives dropped by to greet *los recién casados,* and invited us over for dinner.

In the evening, all of us drove to La Plaza de las Delicias. It was the largest town square in Ponce, where El Parque de Bombas, the old fire station painted in vivid reds and oranges, was located. We ate ice cream and I sat on a park bench beside María Elena, observing the well-primped young girls wearing pastel-colored dresses parade around one direction, while the teen-age boys, neatly groomed and sporting summer shirts or *guayaberas,* circled in the opposite direction. Boys ogled the girls and whistled, made kissing noises and released a torrent of compliments: *"mira linda, qué buena estás,* or *me muero si no me miras."* The girls smiled coquettishly and nodded, or looked away with an air of detachment. María Elena told me that when they whispered it meant that secret dates were being planned. Only engaged couples were allowed to stroll openly holding hands. All of this transpired under the watchful eye of adults who spent the entire evening observing and evaluating every move their kids made.

The first evening was tolerable—it was all new and kind of interesting. But by the second night, when I found myself once again sitting on the same bench next to María Elena, I became unbearably bored. I looked over and saw Charlie, Roberto and several other men having the same heated debate they had the night before over the merits of their favorite baseball teams. This was not what I had imagined doing on my honeymoon. I had envisioned romantic tropical sunsets, during which Charlie and I would dance all night and then make love until daybreak.

Instead, there I was watching a bunch of *pendejitas,* marching around doing their little cock-teasing routines. They're just as horny as the guys, I thought. I figured this had to be the most tiresome evening I'd ever spent in my life. In an effort to cheer up, I thought about home and pictured myself at a block party. There I was dancing to a local band, greeting everybody and hanging out with my girlfriends. We were all goofing around and having a ball.

Suddenly, I heard my name. It was Charlie asking if I wanted more ice cream. I shook my head. There was nothing short of leaving this place that would lift my spirits. I felt drained by the monotony of the evening ritual. I was fed up. Tonight, I was telling Charlie.

As if sensing my boredom, María Elena gently tapped my hand and spoke in an apologetic tone. "It's not very lively on week nights. But on weekends we have a marching band playing in the plaza. And next week, Paula, there's going to be a big outdoor dance with a great band coming in from San Juan. You'll have fun, you'll see."

I wanted to shout, BIG FUCKING DEAL, but instead I nodded politely and held my tongue. As far as I was concerned, by next week we'd be history, long gone from Ponce.

Later that night when I confronted Charlie, he became furious.

"What the hell's wrong with you? We just got here! You wanna act like we got no manners and just eat their food, accept their hospitality and then split. No, baby, no. You knew we were coming to stay a while. So, just sit tight for a couple of more days and we'll leave in good time. I promise."

The following day, early on Wednesday, Charlie declared he was off to his reunion.

❖ ❖ ❖

Wednesday night I couldn't fall asleep. Every time I heard a stir or a sound I knew it must be Charlie. I imagined him tiptoeing in sheepishly, getting undressed and laying down beside me. I even heard his familiar soft snore brought on by too much booze. It was all illusion because Charlie never returned that night, nor the next morning either. By Thursday evening, when I sat down to have supper with the Gómez family, my eyes were bloodshot from crying.

I had no appetite and pushed the food from one side of the plate to the other. When Roberto spoke, he was so matter-of-fact that I hardly understood what he was saying.

"By the way, Charlie telephoned me earlier today at work. He said to tell you that he'll be coming back in a day or two at the most, but he's not sure."

My jaw dropped and I stared at Roberto unable to speak.

"*Mira,* Paula, in the meantime, I suggest you just relax. Read a little or just take some time out for yourself—it'll do you good. Tomorrow you might even visit some of our cousins. And you know, of course, that in the evenings you're welcome to go out with María Elena and the kids. Right, María Elena?"

Panic gripped me. What was this fool saying, anyway? Before María Elena could answer, I stood and demanded to know where Charlie was. "You better tell me where my husband is. He should have called me directly in the first place. But right now I need to call him. Understand? So, just tell me where he is."

Roberto shrugged, and when an insolent smirk crossed his lips, I wanted to riot.

"Where the fuck is Charlie? You have to tell me; I'm his wife... *¡carajo coño!* I need to know. God damnit!"

By now María Elena had sent the children out of the room. Roberto sat silently, gaping at me with his mouth wide open. I glared back and waited until he finally responded. "You better calm down, okay? No use in yelling and using dirty language. We have children in this house. Besides, Charlie didn't tell me where he was, and I didn't ask. It's not my business. My cousin married YOU, didn't he? You're his lawful wife, eh? Charlie will come home when he's good and ready. Where do you think you are, Paula? You're in Puerto Rico and NOT in New York City *por allá en el Bronx.* Here we have our values. *Aquí,* men are allowed to release tension. *Machos no son hembras.* You can't boss us and keep tabs on us."

"I'm on MY HONEYMOON. *¡Carajo!* What tension are you talking about? We just got married for christsakes! *Ese cabrón* said he was coming back the next day! That's today. Why? Why is he doing this to me? Besides, this is our honeymoon... MY HONEYMOON."

My shouting evolved into cries, and tears began to spill until I couldn't stop sobbing. "Shit... this is like a stupid joke. I can't believe it," I screamed.

María Elena rushed over to comfort me but I shoved her away.

"For God's sake, take it easy, Paula."

Roberto spoke in a firm voice as if admonishing a child. "Come on, every man needs a little freedom now and then. You don't see my wife busting my *cojones*, do you? Right, María Elena?"

"No," I snapped, wiping my eyes and blowing my nose with a napkin, "that's because she agrees with everything you do or say! God! I'm sick of this town and this awful heat and the boredom. I want to LEAVE. I wanna go home."

"Listen, I'm even more sick of your complaining about Ponce. It's hot here because there are no mountains. Look at a map and learn something. Ponce is in the coastal savannahs... we're an important seaport and a real city." Roberto was getting furious again. "If you want cool air, then go up into the highlands, to Barranquitas in the sticks where your folks come from. *¡Con los jíbaros!* Sure, down here it's hot... but we're cosmopolitan, with streets, traffic, running water, toilets, etcetera, where people wear shoes. And we like it here! We're not *jíbaros* in Ponce. Understand? Sophisticated people get used to hot weather."

"Right," I snickered, and stood up. By now I was beyond furious. "Great big sophisticated Ponce! Tell me where I can grab a bus or a subway and get transportation in a minute? Compared to New York City, Ponce is the sticks, you hear? THIS is a hick town! If my husband was where he should be, instead of being a *macho mamao*, I could go to the mountains or to the freaking MOON, or anywhere, as long as I get the fuck out of here! But he's got the car that WE rented and I DON'T DRIVE. So, what do you think, Mr. Hot-Shot Lawyer-Wanna-Be-Judge? Should I walk to Barranquitas?"

"If you were my wife, I'd really give you something to complain about." Roberto clenched his fists menacingly and moved toward me. I grew up in the South Bronx, and this sucker was wimpy compared to the nasty dudes I knew. I sneered at him and fixed my gaze directly into his eyes, daring him to try something. I had already moved the soup tureen close to me and was prepared to clobber him in an instant. I really wanted to kill Charlie, but at that moment Roberto would do just fine. For a brief moment just before he backed off, I saw terror cross his face. Clearly he realized I wasn't kidding.

"You asshole...," I mumbled, tempted to throw a glass pitcher up side his head. I smiled as he turned and walked off, making much of ignoring me.

After that, I couldn't bear to see anybody and, except for using the bathroom, I didn't leave my bedroom. María Elena kept inviting me to eat, but I refused to budge. Finally, she put food on a tray and left it outside my door. I drank the coffee and juice and attempted a few mouthfuls of food, but I couldn't swallow.

Hour after hour, I lay underneath the mosquito net listening to the sounds that echoed through the house. After a while I became acutely aware of how María Elena was forever serving and attending to Roberto. It seemed that most of the time she was busy complying with his commands. I remembered how at each meal she always served Roberto, even when the platters of food were placed in front of him. When he called out for water, María Elena would stop eating, dash over to his side of the table and pour him a glass. I'd hear her rushing as soon as he stepped out of the shower, "I'm coming, Papi, with your towel and clean underwear..." Roberto's booming voice resounded through their large home, repeating her name, "María Elena, bring me... María Elena, where are my socks? María Elena... you'll make me late! ¿María Elena? ¡Por Dios, AVANZA!"

Periodically, María Elena knocked on my door and timidly asked if she could come in, or if I needed anything, anything at all. I thanked her and sent her away as gently as I could, and then returned to my slow burn.

❖ ❖ ❖

On the third day, Friday, I awoke with a horrible headache. I had just spent another fitful night being constantly startled awake by any common noise—a car being parked, a door being slammed or footsteps coming up the walk.

Minutes later I heard María Elena's familiar knock as she set down my breakfast tray outside my door. After she'd gone off to work, I went to the bathroom and swallowed a couple of aspirins. I drank some juice and finished the coffee, then lay down once more.

During those few days, time held no relevance beyond the sole purpose of waiting. Up until then I'd spent every moment being desperate, but today I was too worn out to despair. I felt completely exhausted and, oddly enough, I was overcome by a sense of quiet, a calmness. I began reflecting and questioning why I was there in that room feeling trapped like a prisoner and helpless, waiting for Charlie to return so he could set me free.

At first, I decided circumstances had created what was happening. Then, I blamed myself for being far away from home. How I hated this town and everyone in it. But I soon reasoned that even back home Charlie's behavior was not much different.

"This time it's Ponce's fault," I muttered in self-mockery. "That's right, Paula, fault this town and the people, blame the country, blame the whole world. How about the goddamn universe being responsible... everything and everyone, except him!"

If Charlie could vanish with such indifference on our honeymoon, I wondered, what would the rest of my life be like... when I'm stuck with a couple of kids? My heart sank as I touched my wedding band. We were legally married and inextricably tied. Parting meant divorce. Immediately, familiar apprehensions surfaced. Without Charlie I'd be all alone once more, like when my parents died. My head started pounding again, and the heat made my body tremble in it's own sweat. I reached over and poured myself a glass of tepid water from the large pitcher on the dresser and drank most of it. After about a half-hour I stopped thinking and finally submerged into deep sleep.

When I awoke and checked my watch, I realized that I had slept for over eight hours, undisturbed by anxious dreams or fearful thoughts. It was the first good sound sleep I'd gotten in days. My whole being felt relaxed. I stretched, slipped on my robe and opened the shutters, drinking in the coolness of the late afternoon breeze. Momentary qualms seized me whenever I recalled that Charlie was still gone. But I had survived his absence and being alone had become a real possibility. I stood before the mirror and studied my own image. My hair was a tangled mess. I looked worn-out. Dark circles framed my eyes, but they were no longer bloodshot. I had not one more tear left to shed over that bastard. I smiled, the crisis was over.

I took a hot shower, shampooed my hair and put on a pretty dress. This evening I had resolved not to argue with my hosts and to make myself useful. After all, it wasn't Roberto or María Elena's fault that Charlie had split, even if they had bestowed him with their blessings.

Supper was usually a simple fare made up of soup or more vegetables and leftovers from the afternoon meal. Usually we ate around seven o'clock in the evening. The woman who cleaned house and cooked the main noon meal was gone by four o'clock, and routinely María Elena prepared supper. This evening she wasn't in the kitchen. Instead I found her working in the laundry room. She was ironing a very clean white shirt.

"I'm sorry, but I must get this shirt as well as the rest of Roberto's clothes ready for this evening. So supper will be a little late tonight. He fusses if I don't have everything ready on time."

I volunteered to cook and baby-sit the kids so that they could both be free to go out for the entire evening.

"Thanks, but no. It's only Roberto who goes out Fridays," María Elena said as she pressed down, forcefully driving the steaming hot iron with a furious energy that smoothed out every tiny wrinkle in the shirt. "I'll only be a little while; I'm almost finished. But...," she hesitated then shrugged and blurted, "you can keep me company, if you're not too angry with me. That would be nice."

I followed her into their bedroom and watched as she carefully fitted the impeccably white, perfectly ironed and heavily starched shirt that resembled a cardboard cutout on to a hanger. She then brought out Roberto's undershirt, shorts and socks, flawlessly washed and ironed, and mindfully positioned them out on the bed. In what appeared to be a well-rehearsed sequence, she removed a lightweight dark blue suit from his closet and brushed the jacket and pants until there was not a particle of lint anywhere. Finally, she brought out his black leather shoes and brushed them vigorously until they shone like mirrors. As I watched María Elena painstakingly select his tie, I figured there was no way Roberto was going out that night with the guys. Such an elegant outfit meant something else.

"There," she said, scrutinizing his outfit to make sure everything was immaculate. "What do you think?"

"I think everything looks fabulous. But that has got to be the whitest and cleanest shirt I've ever seen. I don't know how you do it. Back home we send all of Charlie's white shirts to the Chinese laundry. I could never do such a wonderful job. Honest!"

María Elena beamed proudly, delighted by my praise.

"Do you do this for him every Friday?"

María Elena nodded.

"So, where does Roberto go that he's got to look so very elegant... to an exclusive men's club?"

"He just goes out," she replied, turning away. "Now, it would be nice if we got supper started."

I wanted to ask, where's "out?" But suddenly, María Elena's attitude became formal and distant.

I respected her silence, and for the most part we worked side by side and without speaking. We peeled and sliced plantains and yucca, crushed garlic and chopped onions and fresh cilantro. Once in a while one of us asked the other for some salt, more olive oil, a utensil or a bowl. I was still curious, but said nothing. I could hear Roberto enter and I listened to the familiar sounds as he took a quick shower and went into his bedroom.

We set up a small table on the patio with four place settings. María Elena called the kids in and we all sat down to eat. In the middle of supper, Roberto appeared, meticulously groomed from head to foot. He kissed his children and cautioned them to behave and listen to their mother.

"See you tomorrow." He spoke in a casual manner as he rubbed María Elena's nape and back. Then he looked directly at me and announced, "Listen, Charlie will probably be back tomorrow. Just hang in there."

Without waiting for my reply, he turned abruptly and swaggered out to the front gate. My heart jumped and I felt a pounding in my chest. For the next few seconds I wanted to run after him and demand that he tell me all he knew. But by the time Roberto had shut the front gate and disappeared, I released that temptation.

After supper, we cleared the dishes and sat on the front porch to enjoy a vista of the long wide tree-lined street. Luz María and Robertito played out in front of their house with other children. It was fun to watch the procession of folks who strolled by greeting their neighbors, some stopping along the way to sit and chat a while. I heard the echoes of voices welcoming visitors and offering *un cafecito* or *un refresco.*

María Elena smiled at me. "I'm so glad you're feeling better. There's nothing like good conversation to pass the time pleasantly. Don't you think so, Paula?"

I nodded, inhaled deeply, breathing in the cool night air. I decided that it was good to be back in the real world.

I told María Elena about life in New York, the Bronx, my job and night school. She listened wide-eyed and said she'd always wanted to visit New York. María Elena was actually born and raised in Sabana Grande, a small town further up toward the mountains. "Where it's a lot cooler than Ponce." She laughed and winked at me.

From grammar school to university, María Elena had attended only Catholic schools. Except for Roberto, she had never even dated another man. "We had kids right away. Now, between Roberto and my children, I have no time for myself. If my mother or two older sisters were here, they'd help out, but no one in my family lives nearby. I really miss them."

When I asked about her girlfriends, María Elena said Roberto disapproved of her having close women friends. "He says he doesn't want me around a bunch of *chismosas*. He can be very possessive. My mother says I'm lucky to have a man who loves me that much. But sometimes I need to talk to someone else I can trust, and that's why I was so glad when you came. I thought maybe we could become good friends."

I took a more careful look at María Elena. She was still slender, very pretty and such a gentle person. As the evening went on, we talked about everything from politics to cooking. Around ten o'clock, María Elena put the children to bed.

I sat on the porch and mused on about what an elegant old city Ponce really was, with its stately eighteenth and turn-of-the-century homes and tree-lined streets. "Fuck Charlie," I sighed, and decided that the next day I'd go exploring. I'd also check out transportation that could take me up to Barranquitas. I knew my mother's sister lived there. In fact, I planned to look up all of my *jíbaro* relatives.

María Elena returned with two glasses and a pitcher of cold lemonade. She reached over and gently stroked my hair.

"I'm sure Charlie'll be home very soon, probably tomorrow. You'll see. Men," she said sadly, and sat back in her large wicker rocker. "Well... that's just the way they are. They're free to go anywhere and do as they please while we suffer. That's our lot in life."

"Where does Roberto go on Fridays? Come on, tell me," I urged. "You brought up the subject of men just now, not me. Charlie goes out every Friday night with the guys. No matter how much I complain, he insists it's his right. I thought that our honeymoon would be different, but as you can see... Now, you tell me about Roberto. I promise I won't say a thing. Honest."

"He goes to see his *corteja*, his other woman, every Friday without fail. She has a child by him. A little boy, Miguel, who's five now. He resembles my Robertito."

María Elena said it didn't matter who she told because everybody in Ponce knew. "Her name is Adriana. She lives way over at the other end of town."

Her words felt like cold water cascading down my back. After the initial shock, I was overcome by emotions of betrayal, helplessness and anger.

"Why do you bother to clean and press his shirts and clothes when you know he's going to be with her... like, in her bed? I mean, Roberto looked immaculate, like he could be going out to hunt for chicks. And he was dressed to kill, by you! Yeah me, personally, I wouldn't care if that motherfucker went out bare-assed with his balls exposed!" I was trying to keep my voice down, but at that moment I couldn't restrain my contempt for María Elena. "I can't accept that you're that big of a FOOL... I really can't!" I began to understand why this woman was incapable of being on my side, and my rage intensified.

"And, don't be including me in your sorority of suffering sisters. Don't! You're the sucker, not me. I'm not joining your club of super *pendejas*. Just tell me why, María Elena... WHY, coño!? Don't you have any pride? I'd be fucking furious!" After a moment of silence that seemed endless, Maria Elena gathered up the courage to reply. "You don't understand, Paula. This is not New York. Here, we do things differently."

"Really? Is there a law here that says wives must polish their husbands shoes and dress up their husbands in super-clean clothes so that they can be allowed to spend the night in their mistresses' bed? Or can't he fuck her wearing a dirty shirt? I understand now why Charlie thinks he can dump me in this place, then go out and do anything he feels like. Now it's clear, coño... he believes I have no rights. THANK YOU!"

I glared accusatorially at María Elena. Intimidated and stupefied, she shrank back. I had seen and heard enough. As I turned to leave she blocked my path.

"Wait... Paula, no, wait." María Elena's voice trembled and she fought back tears. "You have a lot to learn about life for women here. It's true, compared to men, we haven't the same kind of rights. But I can tell you that not all women here do what I do. I have my own personal reasons, you see, and I do what I have to in order to keep harmony in my family. I live in a tight-knit community where everyone knows everybody else's business. People talk, people gossip. And, I will not allow anyone..." María Elena paused, took a deep breath, straightened her shoulders and stared defiantly at me, "... anyone to accuse me of being less than a good and decent wife. I do have my dignity, you know. Oh, yes!

"If my husband must go to Adriana—and I know I can't stop him, because believe me I've tried for years and to no purpose, then he's going there with clean underwear, polished shoes, a perfect suit and the cleanest, whitest shirt that woman will ever see. My husband will be dressed impeccably from head to toe. No one... and, I repeat... NO ONE is ever going to call me a pig, or dirty, or inadequate in my obligations. I may not have control over what Roberto does, but I do control my own duties. It is a matter of pride!"

I almost asked if she was jesting. But I quickly saw this was no joke. María Elena meant every word. She was quite indignant, upset and about to burst out crying. I was stunned by the pitiful sight of this woman, who was at least ten years older than me, educated and intelligent, attempting to defend her reputation with so much hubris. Her major defense, that she endured being a devoted servant to an unfaithful and abusive husband, left me speechless.

After a few minutes of silence, I told her that I was tired and needed to sleep. Inside my room with the door tightly shut, I was able to ignore the muffled but disturbing sounds of María Elena's crying.

I lay down on the large four-poster bed that had been my shelter for those past few days and closed my eyes. Images and feelings of all that had happened since my arrival surfaced: Charlie leaving, my incessant crying and my extreme fear of being all alone. Whenever I replayed María Elena's words in my mind, I didn't know whether to laugh at such ridiculous behavior or weep in sympathy. At other moments I was outraged at María Elena's lack of self-esteem. But overall, pity prevailed when I remembered María Elena's staunch defense and her ludicrous sense of pride.

My honeymoon trip to the island of "paradise," where my parents longed to be buried, had upset my marriage. But for all of my sorrow and the impending upheaval, I was also given the gift of choice. I could stay with Charlie, perhaps for the rest of my life, or I could embrace my personal freedom and go on alone.

That night for the first time, it became obvious that living with Charlie meant I'd always be wondering where he was and who he was sleeping with. It meant checking the clock for his return and hoping he still loved me enough to come back. Loving him, being loyal and faithful to our union, nothing I could do would ever mitigate the reality that I had been born female. Consequently, I understood without a shred of doubt that Charlie would always consider me his inferior.

I undressed, switched on the overhead fan and put out the lights. The sweet smell of jasmine floated in through the shutters and I heard the song of the tiny *coquis* serenading the island. My marriage vows seemed to have been taken so long ago. Promises that were no longer real.

I turned off the table lamp and shut my eyes. A peacefulness settled over me and I smiled, excited by the many possibilities my choice would bring.

❖ ❖ ❖

The next day when Charlie returned, he meekly handed me a necklace of sea shells. He was astonished when I nonchalantly accepted his gift without comment. Immediately, he went into a long convoluted explanation.

"Mira, baby, you know how guys are. My old buddies refused to let me go... I mean, after all, we ain't seen each other in years. I explained that I had my beautiful young wife waiting at home. Man, like I'm on my honeymoon, I kept pleading. But you know, a few more drinks, a couple of card games and one thing led to another..."

I barely listened. It was the same old Charlie, frantic with guilt and babbling bullshit. I could smell his sweat mingled with the distinctive odor of sex. That pig had been with another woman and didn't even bother to wash properly. Midway through his litany of apologies, I told him to save it.

"Listen, I don't wanna hear any more excuses, okay? What's done is done. So, let's put all of that shit behind us. Because this is MY vacation, too. Between my job and night school, how often do I have time off? Never! So, let's forget about all that *mierda* that just went down. The only way you can make it up to me is by meeting my demands. No more of your bullshit on this trip. You had your fun, right? Now it's my turn to have a good time and enjoy the days we have left. Here's what I want..."

I outlined my plans for the rest of our trip. We would leave the next day right after breakfast, then drive up to Barranquitas. After a day or two with my relatives, we would head out to San Juan for the remainder of our vacation.

Charlie agreed without a whimper of protest. I could see he was grateful that I had spared him a hard time. He was expecting my tears, recriminations and threats. I figured his guilt would guarantee that I'd get my way for at least the rest of our trip.

Charlie thanked me repeatedly for being so understanding. "Baby, I thank my lucky stars that nothing's really changed between us. I still got my young, beautiful and loyal wife. I am one lucky son-of-a-bitch!"

On Monday, as we said our good-byes, María Elena took me aside. "I hope you still like me, Paula, and that you understand my situation."

I assured her that even if I never understood her situation or her behavior, I still liked her very much.

"You're young, Paula. Wait until you have your own family. You still have a lot to learn."

"Oh...," I put my arms around María Elena and gave her one long last hug, "but I have learned. I've learned a whole lot already, honest! María Elena, you're a better teacher than you think. Make no mistake about that."

I sat beside Charlie as we drove off and I chuckled, because it had become so clear to me that this man was already long gone for me. One day even his ghost would be wiped away.

"What's so funny, baby?"

"It's got to do with the cleanest whitest shirt I ever saw." By now I was giggling loudly.

"Share your joke girl, so I can laugh, too."

"You wouldn't understand."

"Try me."

"It's no use, Charlie, I promise."

"You women... I give up."

"Yeah."

As the car headed up toward the highlands, I looked back at the sprawling, peaceful city of Ponce and experienced an odd sense of nostalgia. Somewhere deep in my psyche I knew that no matter how long I lived or how many unforeseen turns my future would take, I'd always recall this singular place, where my transformation from girl to woman came to pass.

❖❖❖

In Another Place in a Different Era

Although I had arrived twenty minutes ahead of time, I fixed my gaze at the entrance, hoping Joaquín Thomas would come early. Joaquín and I had been living together for eight months and planned to get married early next year. Tonight we were having our own private celebration to seal our commitment. The Alsace-Lorrane was a small restaurant serving French Provincial food, located in the west Forties in Manhattan. I had already ordered an expensive bottle of champagne, and it sat in a cooler waiting to be opened.

When she first walked in, I wasn't sure it was Iris, because she wasn't wearing her thick horn-rimmed glasses. This was curious; just last week I thought I'd spotted her walking about a couple of yards ahead of me. I was on 57th Street, heading towards Carnegie Hall to purchase tickets for the following Friday's concert recital by the soprano Victoria de los Angeles. I couldn't get a clear view even from the back because the person was under a large black umbrella, yet somehow I was sure that the diminutive frame and brisk walk belonged to Iris Martínez.

Eager to catch up, I rushed after her, carelessly stepping into puddles and soaking my shoes. Fortunately, she was heading in my direction and I followed close behind until we got to Carnegie Hall. Then, all I saw was her black umbrella vanish as she slipped inside.

The lobby was damp and crowded and smelled of clammy bodies. People held their dripping umbrellas while others came in drenched. I searched along the long line of ticket buyers and among those who had come in to avoid the downpour. No one resembled a short, skinny, pale woman wearing thick horn-rimmed glasses. Perhaps I was mistaken. After all, I hadn't gotten a clear look at the person under the umbrella. I gave up and queued at the back of the ticket line.

Now this evening, here she was again. For twelve years I had not laid eyes on Iris, and only this past week it seemed I had spotted her twice. An unusual coincidence, for sure, although she didn't exactly look like the Iris I used to know. I remembered how she would struggle to keep her hair in place by winding hair bands and placing clips all over her head. Yet tufts of her brown hair always stuck out every which way like soft cotton. She usually dressed in baggy shirts or sweaters and loose skirts or jeans, and wore low pumps or sneakers.

Tonight she was not wearing glasses, and since she was terribly nearsighted I assumed she was wearing contact lenses. Her hair was impeccably cropped in a short, becoming afro. Iris wore a simple double-breasted black suit, large gold hoop earrings, a red silk scarf and black suede boots. No matter how chic she looked, there was no way I could mistake that skinny body all of four feet ten inches with the build of an eleven-year old. Even with her high heel boots she looked petite. It definitely was Iris.

Her companion, a distinguished middle-aged white man with gray hair, was dressed in an expensive business suit. Attentively, he took her coat, gave it to the maitre d' to be checked and escorted Iris to her seat.

Their table was placed by the far wall of the dining room near the windows, and she sat at an angle facing away from me. My table was situated in the no-smoking section on the opposite side on the upper floor level, where I could clearly observe them. He was making quite a fuss over Iris, lighting her cigarette and showing interest in her every gesture. Iris had not yet turned in my direction, so I supposed she still hadn't seen me.

Well, we both had changed in twelve years. I was just twenty-two back then and married to Gerry Garza. Iris was about twenty-nine and living with Dennis, Gerry's older brother. The last time I saw her, she was recovering from the worst beating Dennis had ever given her. Sure, he had beat on her before, but Dennis had never been so brutal.

Now I think back and attribute her lack of self-esteem to the persistent abuse she endured. Iris was convinced she was ugly beyond remedy, repulsive without hope of improvement. These feelings were constantly reinforced by the man she adored and whom she supported, Dennis himself.

Of all the many women Dennis had been with, Iris was the best. She was educated, smart and had a heart of gold. If you needed a few dollars, all you had to do was ask. Many of the folks in the neighborhood owed her money. Most paid her back, but she never hassled those who didn't. As my mom said, she was *buena gente*. Iris worked downtown as a paralegal, was finishing college and wanted to become a lawyer. In spite of her reputation for being unkempt and homely, everybody commented on how intelligent Iris was. "Too bad," Gerry used to say, "she might be smart and have a good job, but she don't know how to dress good. And, she's *bien fea*. Ugly... man what a dog."

It was true Iris appeared less than sexy and unattractive, yet there was also something impish and upbeat about her. She had a vitality in her demeanor, as well as a wonderful smile that lit up her face, and I thought all that was downright appealing. I figured those grotesque glasses she wore and the way she dressed contributed to making her appear homely. But whenever I suggested that she wear nicer clothes and use contact lenses, she'd always say no.

"I don't have money to spend on fancy clothes. And I already have contacts, just can't get used to them. They tire my eyes when I read for long periods.

Besides, I like it when people say my glasses are bigger than I am and that's how they know it's me who's coming. My horn-rimmed glasses are my trademark."

I speculated that by hiding behind those ostentatious glasses, she was telling the world, "Look, I may not be pretty, but I am intelligent."

It was a surprise to everyone when those two started going together because Dennis Garza usually picked pretty women who were shallow thinkers, witless, and who had little ambition. And, he was also a handsome, handsome guy. At one time I thought he was one of the sexiest men I'd ever met. I wasn't the only one to say so, either.

"There's nothing outstanding about him," my sister Rachel had once said. "Like he ain't real tall or nothing. It's like the way he's put together, all the pieces are perfect, especially that smile."

Dennis stood medium height, had dark, shiny, curly hair, brown eyes with long lashes, smooth light-olive skin and a set of very white straight teeth. When people first met Dennis he appeared affable and gentle. He had a way of cocking his head boyishly, grinning and somehow appearing like a guileless adolescent. Dennis easily pretended to be an interested listener by staring at you wide-eyed, as if impressed by every word you spoke.

Actually, Dennis Garza was neither guileless nor concerned. He was a vain, selfish man capable of great cruelty and violence. In fact, he had gotten a few unfortunate girls pregnant and quickly abandoned them. People said he was the father of several children in the neighborhood whom he refused to acknowledge as his own. He never held down a job, was always in debt and caused his parents a great deal of grief. Dennis was his mother's favorite and he could twist her around his little finger. More than once he had taken her rent money without an ounce of remorse.

"This boy'll be the death of me," she'd say, and no one would contradict her.

Dennis prided himself on the way he could con his way into women's hearts. It was a sport with him. He'd live off his women, take all their money and, when there was nothing more to be gained, he'd dispose of them like worn-out garments. That's why it didn't take long before he began to live exclusively off women.

"It's easy," he bragged, "and comes naturally because I give the broads what they need."

Up until the age of about fourteen I had a crush on Dennis. So did Rachel and the rest of the girls in my neighborhood. Then one day I was in my bedroom and overheard him talking to my brother Frankie, who sometimes hung out with Dennis, hoping to make out with one of the women he had discarded. The two of them were in the living room gossiping and bragging.

"Women ain't nothing but cunts, man. All you have to do is say you love them and they fall right into your bed. They don't care if you mean it or not. *Ay, papi, dime que me quieres.*

"Bitches love to be bossed around, too. Just give them a few serious slaps when they don't behave. Then fix them with your magic wand and tell them all that love bullshit they wanna hear. And you got it made, bro."

From that time forward, I had a sincere dislike for Dennis Garza. When I married his brother, Gerry, it was all I could do to tolerate Dennis' presence.

Now, as I recollect, Iris was the smartest woman Dennis ever had. Dennis was crafty and knew how to swindle and get over, but intellectually he was dense. After high school I don't believe he ever read anything but sports, and tits and ass magazines. Once, after Iris had endured yet another nasty whipping, I asked her why she accepted his abuse.

"You are so smart, Iris. Why don't you leave that mean bastard?"

"I don't care what people think or say," she told me, wincing in pain. "I got the handsomest guy around. Dennis Garza is my man and he loves me. Me, ugly little Iris."

That was when I understood that his stupidity and reckless abuse didn't matter, because Dennis' deception had convinced her she was loved and that the ugly duckling had conquered the beautiful prince. Iris was bewitched.

During their three years together, her entire life revolved around Dennis. In her judgment he could do no wrong. Every two weeks Iris handed him her paycheck and he gave her an allowance. She made a home for him, took care of his clothes, cleaned and cooked for him. He continued to cheat on her with no thought to discretion. When she protested or complained, he beat her. It was common to see her walking around with bruises or a black eye. Yet Iris accepted her physical and emotional wounds and remained loyal.

On occasion when he was in a good mood, Dennis tossed her a compliment in the way one might speak to a pet. "Iris Martínez, you're some homely bitch, ugly as a toad, but you're my baby. I love my toad, my sweet Mami." Iris would smile and bask in his words, grateful for any kindness he offered her.

❖ ❖ ❖

Usually, I kept my distance and wanted nothing to do with them as a couple. Then one day, because of my Aunt Dora's generosity, all four of us spent a weekend together. My Aunt Dora and Uncle Felix had *una casa de campo* and seven wooded acres in upstate New York, near the town of Poughkeepsie. It was about a two-hour drive from the South Bronx where we all lived. All of our family helped my aunt and uncle improve their country cottage by building extensions to accommodate more people and by planting fruit trees. In the warm months my relatives even raised chickens. Although my Uncle Felix would have preferred to live out his old age in the tropical warmth of Fajardo, his hometown in Puerto Rico, this was to be their retirement home. My Aunt Dora insisted that as long as their children and family were in the Bronx, they would remain in New York State. We were all invited to come up and stay for the long Memorial holiday weekend.

"To celebrate the beginning of summer, we're going to roast a whole pig, and your mother is making her wonderful *pasteles* and *arroz con gandules*. There's going to be music, dancing, *una fiesta sabrosa*. Sarita, you gotta be there and you must bring Gerry's brother Dennis and his girlfriend Iris," insisted Aunt Dora. "It's a time for the entire family to get together."

Aunt Dora and my mother loved to cook and see all of their children and grandchildren together. In the typical Puerto Rican clan tradition, no one should be excluded. Food and drink was provided in abundance, and the more folks that came to rejoice in sharing, the better.

As I said, personally I didn't mind Iris at all; she was good people, but being with Dennis was not my idea of fun. By the time we drove over to their apartment on Longwood Avenue, Dennis was already drinking. Dennis became mean and nasty when he drank too much. He and Iris loaded their gear in the car trunk and settled in back. It was a Friday evening, and the roads were crowded with traffic heading out of the city. Driving was slow, almost bumper to bumper. Dennis pulled out a fifth of Scotch.

"Here." He shoved the bottle toward Gerry. "Take a drink bro, ease your driving." Gerry glanced my way furtively. I shook my head emphatically.

"No drinking and driving, Dennis," I told him. "Gerry's gotta concentrate. We don't want an accident."

"I ain't talking to you, Sarita. I mean, I respect that you're my brother's wife and all. But excuse me, I'm talking to Gerry. Let him answer. Come on bro, take a small swig..."

"No!" I was furious. "He's driving!"

"Hey! *Qué falta de respeto.* I'm talking to the man here. Show a little respect," Dennis sneered. "Too bad, but my little brother's henpecked," he mocked, and pointed to Gerry. "Look, Iris, my *hermanito* Gerry's wearing *pantaletas!*"

I began to feel uneasy because Gerry and I were always feuding over his claims that I wanted too much freedom. He criticized my option to dress as I pleased, would not allow me to learn how to drive our car and forbade me to ever contradict him in public. All of this had recently become major issues since my enrollment in night school at New York University. Although I didn't know exactly what I wanted to do yet, go into law, history or another specialty, I was definitely going on to higher education. Gerry worked as a municipal bus and train inspector. A good job with benefits, hospitalization, retirement, a job most guys would kill for, he frequently reminded me.

From the start, my attending college had infuriated Gerry. Just that morning he began his harangue about my being out four evenings a week. Why did I have to be better than him? he chided.

What was I trying to prove, anyway? Who, he insisted on questioning, was going to wear the pants in his family?

"I can't believe your old lady won't even let you take a sip of Scotch," Dennis kept goading. *"Bendito,* Iris, are you seeing how sad things are for ole Geraldo?" Whereupon Gerry reached out and Dennis promptly handed him the bottle. He put it to his mouth and took a long pull.

"Not a word," Gerry said, giving me a defiant look. "Don't say shit."

As we drove on, the brothers passed the bottle back and forth, stopping only to ask if either Iris or myself wanted a swig. Each time, we both refused. Traffic was flowing slowly and it looked like the two-hour trip was going to be about twice as long. I glanced back at Iris, who appeared terrified.

Instinctively, I turned on the radio and tuned to a popular salsa music station, hoping to cheer us up. Iris and I began to prattle on about music and what singers and bands we both preferred: Blanca Rosa, La Lupe or Celia Cruz, Tito Puente or Ray Barretto. Our conversation remained idle, yet neither of us wanted to stop. It was as if the sound of our own voices provided some sort of veiled shield against the menacing Garza brothers. After what seemed an interminable amount of time, Dennis gave Iris a violent shove.

"God, what a bunch of gabby hens, right, Gerry?"

As soon as Gerry agreed, Dennis slapped Iris across the back of her head, shouting, "So then shut the fuck up, bitch!"

Iris encased her arms over her head and cowered in the corner.

"Listen, why don't we stop for something to eat," I said, desperate to avoid what I already knew was about to happen. "I'm starving."

At first Gerry was reluctant. He wanted to make driving time, but I also insisted on going to the bathroom. We stopped at a diner, ate some hamburgers and drank coffee. Dennis had a coke, refusing coffee.

I took Iris aside and explained that I planned to ride in back. "He may try to hurt you. But if I'm beside you, he'll back off."

"Dennis is very drunk," she whimpered, and nodded like a frightened child. "They finished the bottle, but Dennis has another fifth of Scotch with him." I told Gerry I was very tired and wanted to sleep. I went in back with Iris while Dennis took my seat up front.

Within a few miles, Dennis was pulling from the second bottle. I was relieved when Gerry refused to join in, claiming he was already high and preferred to concentrate on driving. That was when Dennis started on Iris.

"You are such an ugly bitch. I don't know what I see in a toad like you. Your mother must have been married to that Quasimodo, or Quasifeo. You know, the hunchback of Notre Dame. No, wait... I know, SHE was the hunchback of Notre Dame." His diatribe was unrelenting. "Do you all know that this bitch barks for me when I ask her? Go on, Iris, show 'em. Bark for us, bitch. Bark. Wuff, wuff. Bow, wow... grrr. I whip her skinny butt with my belt; she whines and yelps. Go on, show us how you cry for Daddy. Ouch, geez, ooooh, ouch... gee. Show them, you ugly mongrel..." As Dennis reached in back to slap Iris, I slid in front of her.

"Cut it out!" I shouted. "Gerry, tell him to stop it."

"Stay out of it, Sarita," Gerry warned me. "It's not our business." But he did tell Dennis to stop. "Come on, man, quit it! I'm trying to drive and my old lady's sitting back there. Have some respect."

Dennis would quiet down for a few miles, then he'd turn, grimace at Iris and start his invective. "Do you know that this motherfucking bitch has one tit larger than the other? Imagine having to make love to two different tits on the same skinny body. I'm fucking a freak. She's a freak show... come on, Mami, show them. Take out your tits!" All of this time Iris sat recoiled in a corner, crying silently. Once in a while she wiped her eyes and blew her nose. When I tried to comfort her, she shook her head and gently pushed me away.

"This bitch went and got pregnant on me. I bet nobody knew that, right? Then she wanted to have the kid. No way! She got an abortion because I told her, do you think that kid's gonna come out with my beautiful looks? You too ugly... I can't take no chances on fathering no freak and..." It was then that Iris interrupted Dennis.

"You're a miserable motherfucker," she rasped. "You bastard! Motherfucker, I hope you die! I hope you die!" Dennis turned and, with an incredulous stare frozen on his face, moved his lips but remained mute. After a few moments, he finally bellowed, "You just cursed my mother! Did you hear the bitch, Gerry? She cursed our mother. Nobody in this world curses my mother. Nobody. Shit, my mother's a saint. *Una santa.* A fucking saint!"

The rest of the trip lasted for about another hour, during which time Dennis kept on working himself into a rage, repeating how he was going to whip Iris. "I'm gonna beat your ass so bad, *puta,* that you're gonna wish you was never born. There's gonna be none of you left after I get through with you..."

❖❖❖

The second I recognized the familiar road leading to Aunt Dora's, I began to plan how to get Iris away from Dennis. I poked Gerry and whispered that we had to do something. "I'll grab Iris and make a run for the house. You deal with Dennis." He nodded and gestured that he was with me.

As we drove up the path, Gerry screeched the car to a halt, jumped out and went over to block Dennis. I swung the door open, grabbed Iris and shouted, "Run to the house!"

Iris stepped out, shoved past me and, swinging an empty bottle of Scotch, ran toward Dennis, who was struggling to free himself from Gerry's hold.

"Bastard, motherfucker, I'll kill you!" Iris screamed as she swung full force, barely grazing Dennis' forehead and smashing the empty bottle against the car fender.

"*Coño*, you cut me, bitch!" Dennis wailed.

I had been trailing behind Iris, yelling that she run for cover, and felt myself showered with bits of flying glass. I looked to see that Gerry had also been struck, because he had stepped aside and was busy brushing off pieces of glass that had gotten stuck in his hair.

It took only seconds before Iris and Dennis charged at each other like wild beasts. She clawed and pounded him with her small fists. But she was a sorry match for Dennis. He pummeled Iris like a punching bag, ripped out her hair and locked his fingers so tightly around her throat that I was sure he would strangle the life out of her. It became impossible to separate them.

By now everyone had rushed outdoors and jumped into the scuffle, trying desperately to pry them apart. A free-for-all of bodies, arms twisting, legs kicking, and flying fists, soared across the ground followed by screams that invaded the quiet country night. My mother and Aunt Dora shrieked the loudest, demanding that Dennis had to be stopped. "*¡Por Dios... no!* He mustn't kill her!"

It took everyone's strength to wrestle him off Iris and to finally disengage her. I had suffered a wallop in my left shoulder, Gerry had a bloody nose, and both of us had tiny cuts and scratches all over our faces and arms. Poor Aunt Dora received a nasty bump on her forehead, and my mom had a long and bloody scratch on her forearm.

But it was Iris who was injured beyond recognition. Her face had disappeared under a thick coat of blood, shattered bones and lacerated skin. All the men, about eight of them, jumped on top of Dennis and held him down while we led Iris, who was reeling helplessly, inside the house. My mother, Aunt Dora and some of the other women cleaned her up, put ice packs and raw steak on her face, neck and arms. Aunt Dora gave Iris some of her painkiller pills that had been prescribed for arthritis. My aunt and uncle gave her their bed. The older women took turns tending to Iris all night long.

I lay awake in bed that night beside Gerry, who slept as soundly as a baby. All I could feel for my husband was a void that sank into my chest. I felt utterly helpless. From the minute we got to Longwood Avenue, I had seen Dennis' brutality emerging. Not only had I felt powerless to stop Dennis' abuse, I wasn't even allowed to walk away. I had to stay and listen, to witness and wait, and be a silent participant as another woman was viciously attacked. When my father was verbally abusive, my mother always backed off, appeasing him and apologizing for whatever he accused her of doing or saying.

"Ay, mi hijita, you know how men are. I always keep quiet and let your papa get everything off his chest. That's why he's never laid a hand on me. You have to understand men. They're like little boys who want their own way."

Some little boy, I thought. Dennis almost killed Iris, somebody so small and frail. For the first time in my two years of marriage I understood that I had committed to a man who would never allow me to take charge of my own life.

"No, Mami," I whispered to myself. "I'm not doing it like you. I can't." It was that very night when I first considered a future without Gerry Garza.

The next day I couldn't believe my eyes. Iris' face was puffed up like a balloon and her features were so distorted, it was difficult to figure out where her eyes belonged and if she actually had sockets. Iris' inflamed cheeks and swollen nostrils looked like a pig's snout. Her lips were split open and had the consistency of liver. Several gashes extended from her face down to her neck and arms.

Iris looked so hideous that I burst into tears and began pleading with her to press charges and put Dennis in jail.

"You're a person, a grown woman, not an animal, not his pet slave to abuse and beat!" I was close to hysterics and implored her to have some self-respect. "Have some fucking pride. Stop him from doing this again and send that son of a bitch to jail. I'll testify in court and be a witness. For God's sake, you've got dozens of witnesses." Iris quickly assented that jail was the least he deserved and agreed to go to the police station that very day.

But, Dennis was a professional abuser of women, and he knew how to survive. He feigned remorse and pleaded his case in public. He pointed to the scratches on his own face and told everybody that the worst scratches were in his broken heart. Dennis even asked my Uncle Felix for permission to speak to Iris in everyone's presence. He wept openly and asserted that it would be unjust for her to leave him or to put him in prison.

Then he got down on his knees, kissed her feet, and begged Iris to forgive him. "Mami, you know you're my life. Without you I'm nothing. I'm nobody without my baby. *Te lo juro*, right here in front of everybody. I swear... don't kill me, Iris, don't do this to me. I love you, please, Mami." Dennis smiled his sweetest smile and donned his most innocent bearing.

He didn't fool me for a moment, but Dennis convinced everyone else. They said it was hard to believe that such a sweet and self-effacing guy could be a wicked monster. He should be allowed to show us his good side, was the consensus.

Iris was swayed, and ultimately agreed to forgive him. My family's generosity allowed them to stay on in the country until she got better. Iris took part of her work vacation in order to recuperate in quiet surroundings with Dennis by her side.

I was stunned and dismayed by Iris' behavior. Somehow I had foolishly believed that my words and sentiments had merit and that I could actually help Iris. But instead I was ashamed of my own vulnerability and became even more disgusted with Iris and with myself. I was no one to be giving advice, I thought, not as long as I was still being intimidated by the same kind of abuse that my grandmother and mother had endured.

The following day when I insisted on returning home, Gerry became furious. "We're already here. Let's enjoy ourselves like everybody else. *¿Qué te pasa, coño?* What the fuck's wrong with you, Sarita?"

By now I was too distressed to be bullied, and was quite prepared, if necessary, to take the train home. In the end, Gerry gave in and we left.

The very next day, I got a phone call from my Aunt Dora, telling me that Iris had hemorrhaged and was in the hospital for a few days. My folks had convinced the doctors that she'd been in a car accident. Luckily, she was out of danger now and getting better. Dennis and Iris would be returning to the city the following week, said Aunt Dora.

❖❖❖

Three more weeks passed and I went on with my own life, coping with Gerry's moods and trying to hold down a full-time job and carry nine credits at night. Then one day we received a dinner invitation from Iris. At first I refused to go near them, but Gerry was adamant.

"You always get your way with this college business. Now, you give me some slack here. Dennis is my older brother, I said we would go, so don't be making me look bad." I would never hear the end of it if Gerry went alone. Holding back a heap of adverse feeling, I went.

Remarkably, Iris' face looked almost normal, except for some swollen scar tissue where the stitches were still healing. They were both glad to see us, and Dennis was on his best behavior, obviously still somewhat grateful that Iris had not put his ass in jail. After Iris poured our drinks, she led us into their bedroom and pointed toward the ceiling.

There was a gaping hole of about four to five feet in diameter in the ceiling. "It collapsed in huge blocks." She handed me some Polaroid photos. "See?" Large chunks of cement and lumps of plaster were scattered all over the bed and bureau. "Why, I could have been killed!" Iris chuckled. Then both she and Dennis began to laugh uncontrollably. Gerry and I were perplexed. We failed to see what was so funny.

"This happened the weekend we went to your Aunt Dora's," grinned Dennis. "Now, if I had not given my baby here a little ass-whupping, we wouldn't be able to sue the motherfucking landlord."

"You're suing?" I asked, not believing what was happening.

"Damned straight!" nodded Dennis. "We got a doctor who's cooperating and says Iris has got permanent damage to her vision, and you all know she was already blind! She got partial hearing loss... and what else you got, Mami?"

"Enough to sue for a lot of money," she snickered. I wanted to say something to Iris, like, how can you take money for a bogus accident when it's the man beside you who damaged you in such a vile way. But I was dumbstruck. I barely ate my dinner, anxious to get away from them.

Before I left, Iris called me into the bedroom. "Just some girl talk," she called out to Dennis and Gerry. "We'll be out in a minute." She shut the door. "Look, Sarita. I know you're angry with me."

"No," I shrugged, lying. "Not at all, it's your life, Iris. Do what you want, girl!"

"Never mind, I know you're angry. But listen, I heard you, I heard every word you told me when we were upstate. It's all true." When I pressed her to explain, all she said was, "I can't tell you everything now. I just can't talk about it. But, Sarita, just so you know your words didn't fall on deaf ears. OK?" She gave me a long hug and said nothing more.

A few months later, Iris left Dennis. Disappeared, they said, and no one knew where she had gone. People told me that as soon as Iris received a generous out-of-court settlement from the landlord's insurance company, she split. Some said it was on the very day she got her check. Dennis became so infuriated, he got a piece and went looking to shoot Iris. He searched everywhere—at her work place, in night school—and even harassed her family. But it did him no good. No one saw Iris after that. She seemed to have vanished.

❖❖❖

About a year after she split, I also left Gerry, and two years almost to that day, I got my final divorce papers. I continued my studies, earned a partial scholarship, worked nights and was able to study full-time. Now I'm finishing my doctoral studies at the City University of New York in the History of the Spanish Caribbean. In fact, that's were I met Joaquín Thomas, an associate professor in the Social Sciences Department.

I checked my watch; Joaquín was already ten minutes late. I was tempted to go over to Iris, but felt apprehensive by the sort of greeting I might receive, and decided I'd better not. Instead, I made a quick pit stop in the Ladies Room. As I came out, I heard my name.

"Hi, Sarita." Iris stood before me smiling. "I thought it was you." Shyly, we both hugged. "I told my friend I wanted to speak to you for a few minutes."

She asked if I was alone, I told her about Joaquín, and we chatted at the bar. We spoke briefly about what each of us had been doing for the past twelve years. Iris had become an attorney, and the guy with her was a client who had the hots for her. She wasn't married yet, but she was seeing somebody, another lawyer and it was serious.

"You want to know what happened and why I left Dennis?" she asked as if reading my mind.

I could feel myself blushing and said it wasn't my business. "Dennis killed my baby. You see, Sarita, I didn't have the abortion because I wanted the kid. I thought something that belonged to the both of us would make a difference, would change Dennis. But that night, he beat the child out of me and I had a miscarriage. All the feelings I had for Dennis died with my baby. After that, I couldn't love him any more. It was all over." Iris paused and took a long drag on her cigarette.

"By the time we got back to the Bronx, I had already decided to leave him. And when I saw the damage in the apartment, I asked Dennis to testify that he was there when the ceiling fell on me. You know how good Dennis was at conning people. He used his acting talents well and made a very convincing witness. The insurance company settled out of court. It was wrong to take the money. As a lawyer, I know it's a felony. But I needed to get away, far away from Dennis, and the money gave me a fresh start." She paused and added mischievously, "Anyway, fraud is risky, but Dennis was lethal, right?" We both had a good laugh.

"He thought he was going to get rich from the beating he gave you, so the joke was on him. Dennis deserved far worse for the way he treated you."

"I know…" Iris whispered, then checked her watch and said it was time to get back to her horny client. She asked if I was in the telephone book.

"Yes, I'm living over on West 28th Street now. Call me."

She said she'd do just that. But I knew she would never call.

Reminiscences of beatings and humiliation at a point in time that once linked us both to the Garza brothers were memories neither of us wanted to recall. In these past twelve years we each transformed our lives. Iris and I had traveled on to another place in a different era.

I saw Joaquín enter and headed back to my table. He apologized for being late, then inquired about the person I was speaking to. I told him it was a passing acquaintance from a long time ago. When Joaquin asked what we had talked about, I assured him that it was inconsequential.

"Just girl talk. Now let's order before we open the champagne. I'm starving!" We picked up our menus and proceeded to order dinner.

❖ ❖ ❖

My Newest Triumph

Usually before a large solo exhibition, I'd be battling with my fears of rejection by the public and worrying over the possibility of bad reviews. Tonight, instead of anticipating dire consequences, I was experiencing a mood of euphoric optimism.

During the past two weeks, Emma and I had been communicating on the telephone, long distance, almost every day. This evening we were discussing final arrangements for my one-person art exhibition. It was to be held in three days time at the Angelica Gallery, one of the most prestigious galleries in Old San Juan, and I was excited. All of my etchings, lithographs, silkscreens and pen and ink drawings had already been matted and framed.

Emma Ruiz-González was a journalist, highly respected and acknowledged in the Caribbean. She was my contact in Puerto Rico and was handling the publicity, advertisements and flyers. Emma told me the dealer, Pablo Cortez-Mueller, eagerly awaited my arrival so we could hang the exhibit.

"Great," I responded, and felt loved and cherished by friends and respected by my peers. Now, I was more confident than ever that my show would be a great success. Then I heard his name ring out loud and clear. In the next second I was so stunned my mind went blank, as if I had just been struck unconscious.

"Hey! Hello... Hello? Inez, are you still there?" I heard Emma's voice, but I remained mute. When I recovered I figured I must be in some state of shock, because even after twenty-five years, the mere mention of his name could devastate my emotions.

"Hello, Inez. Please answer if you're still there," Emma insisted. "Is anything wrong?"

"No, I'm here. I'm still here, go on."

"He said you were once friends and he knew your family when you were a kid in New York City, back in Washington Heights. You might recall a Joseph Batista, he said, and that for sure you'd know who Joe was. This guy was very persistent about coming to the reception. He even asked for the name of your hotel. I told him that you were staying at my home and that he was welcome to call there and schmooze about old times."

Emma paused, and when I hesitated, she realized I was troubled. "Inez, are you upset? I mean, do you remember him? Do you even know this Joseph Batista?"

"Yes, I do. I did know him, Emma. I mean a long, long time ago. When I was seventeen years old I married Joe Batista. Our marriage was a disaster and only lasted about a year. I left him. Several years after we parted I filed for an annulment. I haven't laid eyes on him for twenty-five years. Anyway, Emma, that relationship was so long ago I forgot it had ever happened."

I explained the reason she hadn't known about him was because I never spoke about this episode. Not even to best friends, like her. For me it was a dead issue.

"This Joe character's not the father of your daughter is he?" I could hear Emma's surprise and confusion.

Thank goodness he wasn't, I assured her. In spite of my attempts to seem unconcerned I felt insecure and apprehensive about what I might reveal and began to choose my words carefully. Under no circumstances did I want to acknowledge that Joe still held any purpose in my life, and I tried to sound calm. But Emma wasn't convinced.

"Do you want me to call this guy and tell him not to come? I can disinvite him. The reason he contacted me was because I wrote a column about volunteer work done by community organizations. I mentioned him only because he was the spokesperson for the Rotary Club. That's our only connection. When he saw your picture and read my piece in the paper about your exhibit, he called me.

"Let me emphatically assure you, Inez, this guy can be told not to come near your exhibition. And, he won't dare mess with me! He knows my power as a journalist. I can easily write a nasty piece about him."

"No!" I exclaimed. "Don't!" The last thing I wanted was for Joe to suspect that he still had any power over me. "No, Emma, thanks. Please, just let it be. I'll handle it and we'll talk some more when I see you in P.R. tomorrow." I reminded her that I had to catch an early morning flight out of JFK Airport and needed my rest in order to sort all this out.

As I put down the receiver, I felt seventeen again and nobody's child. When I lived with Joe Batista, he used to play mind games and exercised threats and violence to dominate my life and impede all of my efforts at independence. Every day when I awoke by his side, I felt alone, powerless, frightened, trapped. All my hopes and dreams of being an artist were forbidden to me by Joe. But I continued with my plans in secret and with great care kept that part of my life hidden away from him.

When my phone rang I jumped, terrified. Was it Emma calling back? Or would Joe dare telephone me at my home? On the third ring I lifted the receiver, placed my palm over the speaker, and listened. A voice on the other end asked for a Reverend James Watkins.

"There's no one here by that name." My voice trembled. I hung up and sat wondering and thinking about stuff from way back. Things I thought I had stored away for good.

When I was five my father died, and six years later, just after my eleventh birthday, my mother died, too. My only brother Frankie was seventeen, old enough to join the Air Force and leave all that calamity behind him. I went to live with my mother's sister Ofelia, my closest relative. Two people could never be more different. My mother was kind and generous to a fault. Aunt Ofelia was mean spirited by nature and miserly. Her husband, Generoso Vasquez, avoided his complaining wife, whining daughter Diedre, and excessively spoiled son Papo, by working as a merchant marine. He would be gone for months on end.

I was always considered a burden and an extra mouth to feed in the Vasquez household. Punishments abounded: I was beaten, locked in closets, deprived of food and made to do most of the household cleaning. On rare occasions, Diedre, who was my age, helped out. Papo was four years our junior and the apple of his mother's eye. He was expected to do nothing. At age eleven he reached pubescence and learned to masturbate. Papo took his newfound skill to heart and at every opportunity busied himself practicing.

As the years passed, I found a refuge in my artwork. That was an area the Vásquez family could not touch. My ability to draw gave me a feeling of independence and self-fulfilling joy that set me apart from them. My talent became an area where they had no power over me. From the time I was very little my mother had acknowledged my talent and frequently counseled that I go on to study art —and make an important contribution to the world and really be somebody—she used to say. So, I knew even then that I was an artist and it made me quite special.

Often at night when I lay in bed, I'd fantasize killing them all. I would imagine committing murder with my bare hands, using whips and baseball bats, or poisoning their food. I made careful detailed drawings of these fantasies and took pleasure and comfort in this secret artwork. My long-term ambition was to become a famous artist, but first I had to find a way to escape from the Vasquez house of horrors. When Joe Batista arrived on the scene, he seemed like the perfect solution.

Joe Batista was thirty, had his own apartment, a car, and was studying for a promising career as a lawyer. When he asked me to marry him, my answer was, yes, thank you. I envisioned my marriage as a trail leading to freedom, far from my pernicious relatives. More importantly, I was sure matrimony would enable me to attend art college and bring me closer to my calling. Our courtship had been brief, less than four months, and after a week's honeymoon, I began life as a married woman.

My new husband was almost as stingy as Aunt Ofelia and he was also possessive and insanely jealous. I had to account for every penny I spent and have his approval on the way I dressed. This was a sorry disappointment, but I was used to unfairness. Somehow an inequitable husband still seemed easier than an entire unethical family. However, when Joe unconditionally forbade me to study art, I knew I faced a precarious situation.

The salary from my daytime job as a clerk-receptionist paid for my share of the bills at home. Car fare, clothes and personal needs used up the rest of my meager income.

Without Joe's knowledge, I had registered at the Art Students League. I desperately needed a second job to pay for my courses and art supplies. Luck blessed me and I was offered a part-time modeling job at the League. At first I felt embarrassed posing nude in front of strangers. But as a student myself, I also knew we were all there to learn anatomy. I soon lost my shyness. Although modeling was tiring work, I was very happy for the extra money and accepted as many hours as I could handle.

All of my receipts from the Art Students League were kept in a plastic shopping bag hidden behind the drain pipes in the kitchen cabinet under the sink in our apartment. Safe, I thought, from the eyes of my nemesis, Joe Batista.

Joe had matriculated as a law student in night school and carried a full load of courses. Most nights he was gone. I was essentially free to arrange my new life to benefit my goals. For months, with care and clever deception, I held down a second job and continued with my studies.

All Joe knew about my artwork were the land-scapes and still lifes of flowers that decorated the walls of our apartment. As far as he was concerned,

I was a dutiful wife, content to stay at home and obey her husband.

There was little joy in my marriage. I somehow managed to cope with Joe's jealous rages, his miserly nature and his attempts to hit me. Like the time I refused to hand over my paycheck. As soon as he came at me with clenched fists, I grabbed a flat cast iron grill and prepared to whack him as hard as I could. I kept my salary and on that day managed to foil his violent attempt. Unfortunately, I couldn't always avoid a blow or a smack.

This occasional physical abuse did not compare to the more frequent verbal torment that I was forced to endure. Joe would order me to sit quietly and attend to his every word. He'd circle around me and point his finger, gesturing his displeasure. His favorite invective was 'nobody's child.' These rebukes rarely varied in context or style. And, when I closed my eyes I could still hear his repeated admonitions:

> Your Aunt Ofelia couldn't wait to marry off her little orphan to a sucker like me. Where's your loving brother Frankie? He don't even write or want nothing to do with you. And, you know why? Because you're one selfish bitch. Always thinking about yourself. I saw you looking at that guy that lives downstairs in the front apartment. Don't think I'm not watching. No more tight skirts either, so you can show your ass off in public.

But you see, Inez, that no matter how you act, I'm the only person in this whole fucking world who really loves you. You hear? Without me you're nothing. Nobody's child! I gave you a home and I take care of you. In fact you could do very good in life and reach your goals. But you keep on trying to challenge my ways and one day you'll be old and all alone. That's when you'll remember that Joe Batista loved you more than anyone on this earth will ever love you. Never, ever forget that without me... you're nobody's child. Remember that!

I learned to tolerate his harangues by focusing on a painting I was working on and considering whether it needed more cerulean blue or hunter green in the background. Perhaps I could alter the position of the torso and improve the overall composition of the piece. My work provided an invisible wall that protected me from the tirades of Joe Batista. Once again, it became my refuge.

What brought our marriage to an abrupt end occurred on a night when I was posing nude. I was preoccupied about applications for scholarships that I had recently submitted to New York University, Pratt, and Cooper Union. The possibility of being granted an endowment to attend college was of great concern. Because how would I explain such a bequest to Joe, I pondered.

But what I didn't know was that quite by accident while Joe was searching in the kitchen for a bottle of shoe polish, he had already discovered my applications and art school receipts. And, he knew just where to find me.

I heard a commotion and looked up to see Joe standing before me reeling and gaping with disbelief. Before I could duck, he lunged forward and grabbed a fistful of my long hair. He smacked me so hard that I flew across the room, bashing against easels and stools before landing on the floor.

Every male student, including the instructor, sat on top of Joe so he wouldn't attack me. He struggled and pleaded that he be allowed to take his wife home.

"... I got every right... she's mine," he whined.

Finally, the police came and I was able to put on my clothes and sneak out with Aldo, another student with whom I had been having an innocent flirtation. That night and for the next couple of weeks, Aldo provided me shelter. Predictably, we became lovers, spent a few months together and parted as friends.

Joe wouldn't give up and proceeded to stalk me for the next year or so. He took a part-time job hacking in order to drive his cab around the city in a desperate attempt to find me. He threatened friends and family, but they didn't know where I was either. A few times he stationed himself outside my job, harassing me. Almost always I had to quit and find other employment.

But by now nothing could ever make me go back. I was in sync with my creative existence and I vanished into the world of artists. It was a space where Joe would never think to search. He hunted in the old neighborhoods, looking for his frightened, powerless wife. But that Inez was long gone; she had been absorbed into a community where creating visual miracles by drawing, painting and print-making had become her life's work.

❖ ❖ ❖

By age twenty-one, my life was on a creative path. I was a sophomore, attending Cooper Union on a scholarship and working to pay for my own small apartment. Finally, I filed for an annulment and contacted Joe. That was when we had our last confrontation.

At the restaurant, the waiter stood guard, ready to interfere if Joe Batista went beyond pounding his fists on the table. Joe had gawked at me incredulously after I conclusively agreed with his accusations of my infidelities during our marriage. But what was driving him to violent indignation was when I informed him that I was not a virgin when he married me.

Joe shrieked that he was the first man to have had me and warned that I had better not play games with him. But I had formulated a plan that would wound his pride beyond redemption and hopefully, rid me of him for good.

On our wedding night Joe had been eager, greedy and immediate. He forcefully penetrated me and I felt the pain pierce into my internal organs. When I saw the sticky mixture of semen and blood in my crotch, I was horrified.

The following morning, exulting in his own power, Joe proudly held up the blood-stained sheets. He had known all along that I was a real virgin and declared that now I was his.

"... Baby, you are mine!" he had boasted.

Now, Joe challenged my new claims because he clearly remembered that I had not even been allowed out by myself without my Aunt Ofelia's permission. He asserted that he was the only man I had dated and the first to ever touch me. Without a doubt he had seen my blood on the bed sheets and rejected my arguments.

But I was resolved to shatter Joe's notion that his virginal conquest had given him the ultimate right to govern my life.

"No, you were NOT the first." I confessed how on our wedding night I had smeared the sheets. "That wasn't even real blood." Joe warned that I had better stop making up stories and held fast to what he had personally witnessed.

But I merely snickered at his naivete and explained how easy it had been to trick him with a little mercurochrome. I confronted him with an arrogance that defied all skepticism.

Following a preamble about my sexual prowess, I went on to invent incidents concerning trysts with older men, usually at the movies or in their cars. Joe continued to express doubts until I elaborated about my seduction of Uncle Generoso.

"I'd force myself on him... then after a while he wanted me."

After that, he appeared genuinely astounded and even inquired if I might be a nymphomaniac and suggested therapy. I replied that sex was my hobby much like other people who collect stamps or play tennis.

"Me... I like sex, lots of sex. In a way, that's my hobby." Why go for therapy when my hobby made me happy, I concluded.

To this day, I wasn't sure if Joe ever really believed me or whether he was simply uncertain. But he began to weep and question if I had ever really loved him. After all of the pain and dread Joe had inflicted I expected that watching him squirm would be my sweet revenge.

Instead, he appeared pitiful and repulsive. Yet, for a brief moment, as he sobbed uncontrollably and called out to God, I was tempted to reach out and comfort him. But I had come this far to earn my freedom and there was almost nothing I wouldn't do to be rid of this man.

Outside in the bitter cold winter, Joe had threatened to kill me, hurled epithets and even made menacing gestures. His last words were:

"You can fucking drop dead for all I care!"

It was a moment of great relief when I saw him rush out of my life all those many years ago. Yet, twenty-five years later, here I was shaking with fear and behaving as if Joe Batista still controlled my life.

Feeling beat, I took a hot shower, finished packing and went to bed. As I lay there I knew I had to face Joe. There was no other way. Despite all of my accomplishments, my marriage to Norman, the joy of having my daughter Carlina, and surviving my subsequent divorce, I had not yet fully resolved my breakup with this man. I'd gone on to live almost an entire lifetime without Joe, and yet the words 'nobody's child' invaded my mind.

It was time to settle accounts so that Joe Batista would get all that was due him.

❖ ❖ ❖

For the next two days I spent most of my time working at the gallery setting up the display and taking care of last minute mundane details. At Emma's I didn't dare answer the phone in case it might be Joe calling. But so far he had not rung up or left a message on her telephone answering machine.

Today was the exhibition and although I was quite prepared for a confrontation if need be, I couldn't help wishing Joe would stay away. Emma and I had arrived early to find Pablo and his busy staff setting out two long elegant tables complete with flower centerpieces and an abundance of fancy cheeses, canapes, tropical fruits and decent wines.

"Maybe he won't come," whispered Emma as if reading my thoughts."

"Who knows?" I shrugged and assured her that I could handle the situation.

Just as we had finished making our final changes, people began filing in. Enthusiastically, I greeted old friends that I'd not seen in years. Soon the gallery was crowded with onlookers. I was pleased that all of my creative labor as a graphic artist for the past two years was being celebrated and shared.

When Pablo announced that we had just sold four etchings and a large silkscreen, I couldn't have been happier. I started to relax, have fun, and forgot all about my impending encounter.

Then I saw a man about eight feet away grinning at me. He was portly, almost bald, and was wearing thick eyeglasses. Immediately I recognized his smile. It was him; it was Joe. The man I had married had a head of thick black wavy hair, large brown eyes with long lashes and was at least thirty pounds thinner than the person that I acknowledged on that day. Paradoxically, his physical transformation made little difference because Joe Batista still emitted the same exact negative energy that he always had.

His stance, grin, the nervous jerk of his shoulders were unequivocal. It was his method of warning that I had better watch my step, or there would be hell to pay later. He smiled at me and waved. My heart began pounding and my insides went cold

with fear. But I inhaled deeply, managed a friendly
nod and continued to interact with my friends, pur-
posely ignoring him.

Joe never approached me. Instead, for the next
two hours he followed me relentlessly, always keeping about a six to ten foot gap between us.

Whenever I turned, he was leering or frowning,
perpetually making yet another grimace exclusively
directed at me. The man who threatened me today
looked like an aging stranger compared to my
young husband of twenty-five years ago. Even
though it seemed uncanny, I was nonetheless experiencing emotional upheavals that belonged to a
time when constant threats and invectives were
common daily occurrences in my life.

Pablo announced that it was time for me to
speak before my public, and informed everyone that
afterwards I would be available to sign the color
catalogs that were for sale.

Having been born and raised in New York City
of Puerto Rican parents, I spoke about my joy at
having a one-person exhibit in my parents' beloved
homeland, and welcomed everyone. People inquired
about my work, and were curious about the variety
of techniques I employed as a printmaker. Others
were interested in the New York City art scene.

At first I saw Joe clearly standing in the center
of the crowd no more than ten feet away, still smirk-
ing and grimacing. He never asked a question or
uttered a word. However, as I answered questions
from the audience I began to enjoy my exchange

with this lively crowd. Everyone was interested and involved. Now and then I'd check out Joe and soon, quite unexpectedly, I lost sight of him. After a while I assumed he'd left.

My talk was over and folks who had purchased catalogs formed a line waiting for me to sign their copies. I sat by the small table taking my time and chatting with each person and inscribing every catalog with my personal greetings.

Finally, Joe stepped up. He was the last person in line and hadn't gone after all.

"How you doing?" He smirked and handed me his catalog. "It's been a hell of a long time, hasn't it?" I greeted him with a brief smile but said nothing. After a long moment, he continued. "You know, my wife said to me, Joe, go to that art exhibit and see if Inez has done any pictures of you. I said, 'Why that's a good idea. You know, baby, the old flame could still be burning.' So, how are you?"

"I'm all right," I answered, and waited.

"Well, you did it, didn't you? Nobody's child became a famous artist after all. You were always a determined person. Hard to tame."

"What's your wife's name?" I asked, ignoring his remarks.

"Just sign it to me. Never mind her. Say, to Joe, an old and dear friend. That's all. You see, baby? I don't ask for much."

I inscribed it -To Joe and his wife, Best Wishes, Inez Otero- and I slipped in my note as well. Joe smiled and cocked his head.

"What's this, a love note?"

"Read it when you're alone," I whispered. "Good luck, Joe, I've got to go."

At that moment Pablo called out to me that I was needed by a client. I told him that I'd be over in a few minutes and lingered on, keeping Joe within my view. I was betting that his ego would keep him hanging around until he read my note. I wanted to see his reaction.

Joe strutted about, briefly glimpsing at my artwork while at the same time directing skulking glances my way. Eventually he ambled over to the side exit, still within my sight.

I saw him open the catalog and pull out the note. As he read my words, his whole body seemed to deflate, much like someone had let out all the hot air in a balloon. My note had been simple and to the point and what he read was:

Yes, you were the first. The blood was real. You were a fool then and you're a bigger fool now.

Before I went to join Pablo and the others, I looked back at the exit once more. Joe had disappeared.

"Forever, this time," I murmured to myself.

"Hey! Inez Otero, you sold two more prints." Pablo beckoned to me. "Come here and celebrate with us!" I joined my guests, held up my glass and proposed a toast.

"To my newest triumph!"

❖❖❖❖

Memories: R.I.P.

After exiting from the Bruckner Expressway, I turned east toward the South Bronx and drove through the streets of my old neighborhood. Everywhere I looked I saw ruins. Nothing appeared familiar. Soon, I realized that I was now a stranger, an unwelcome intruder driving her expensive car through these plundered environs. The empty streets and shattered landscape made me feel like a sleepwalker who had naively stumbled into a precarious situation. And for a moment I considered turning my car around and fleeing, but I was being propelled on in my quest of childhood memories. I had come for a reason and would continue my journey. After all, these streets had once been the center of my universe, and I held on to the premise that I still owned enough street smarts to stay vigilant and recognize danger.

Mounds of garbage were heaped high on empty lots. Broken furniture, rusting metal, and torn plastic bags spilling out rotten food and peoples' leavings formed pyramids of filth and disease. These pyramidal structures created a playground for children and served as survival grounds for stray dogs and cats who were tough enough to compete with the rats.

My barrio, the neighborhood in which I had lived as a youngster, was gone. The lively streets bustling with folks, kids playing as they dodged traffic, the bodegas, fruit stands, bakeries, luncheonettes, beauty parlors... all had been reduced to rubble. In the three decades of my absence it had all vanished. Yet I drove on, hoping to catch a glimpse of a familiar building, a shop, maybe even a person I could recognize.

Foolish woman, I thought. I had experienced a whole new life since my fifteenth birthday; surely I didn't know anyone here anymore.

It was almost eleven o'clock on an exquisite spring morning in early June. The sun shone much too brightly on the ruins. The weather was pleasantly warm, friendly and inviting. People were beginning to sit out on the stoops of the few buildings that remained standing like decaying fortresses holding fast in enemy territory. Children romped through the lots tirelessly collecting old tires, pieces of broken furniture, and inventing new games to play. Jobless men found their usual shady locations. There they banded together, sharing the day's first can of cold beer or a pint of cheap whiskey. Others were busy setting up makeshift tables, preparing for their daily games of dominoes.

I turned onto my old street and headed for my building, where it had all happened, where she had

died and where I had come of age, created my treasured fantasies and swallowed bitter disappoint-
ments. It was also there that I learned to hate my
oldest brother, Manny.

My heart pumped faster when I recognized a
two-story building at the corner, decrepit but still
standing. It was no longer RITCHIE'S TAVERN.
The sign now read TERESA'S BAR AND RESTAU-
RANT. I cruised along ever so slowly and braced
myself for the impact of a clutter of memories.

"Where's one thirty-one," I murmured as I
checked out the numbers on the few remaining
buildings. Then I saw a long stretch of debris surrounded by vacant lots where giant weeds pushed
their way up through the rubble. It was gone! My
building had crumbled down to a pile of red-orange
bricks. I parked my car and turned off the motor.
Except for a sprinkling of people at the corner, the
street was deserted.

I leaned back, disgusted, and shut my eyes,
blocking out the massive destruction. Perhaps this
was all a malevolent dream. I looked again and saw
that the pillage was real. Somewhere hidden among
the debris rested my personal history.

"It's like coming to a fucking war zone!" I shouted
with outrage. I felt cheated and impotent. When I
swallowed, a constriction in my throat developed
into a coughing spasm.

After a few moments I calmed down, examined
my dismal surroundings and remembered the
obsessive memory that had brought me here. Frag-

ments of that dire event when I was just eleven years old had continuously invaded my life. Whether it was during my happiest of moments, or when I was wrestling with self-doubts, the same distressing memory would surface and fill me with shame. The scenes simply emerged without warning just like this morning, at the funeral.

I watched the passing clouds cast shadows over the barren spectacle that spread out toward the horizon. Slowly, I began to concentrate on the bewildering recollections of childhood as they sped through my mind. I focused on that singular evening when I had gone out with my friend Nadia. Soon, exact pictures materialized inside my mind's eye and each image took shape, lucid and precise.

❖ ❖ ❖

I saw my building intact and exactly as it used to be, and I saw myself striding along my active street. At the corner intersection I turned left into the main thoroughfare, replete with movie theaters and small businesses. I mingled with the crowds of busy shoppers.

It was a weekday, and my friend Nadia and I had each gotten special permission from our elders to go to the afternoon double-feature movies. We had promised to get home right after the show. But because we enjoyed the films, a newsreel and a cartoon so much, Nadia and I decided to see the whole program over again. After viewing the main feature for a second time, we checked the clock and agreed we had better get home fast.

Outside, the darkness of the cool autumn evening promptly reminded us that we had blatantly dis-obeyed our folks. It was long past the hour when we were both supposed to be in our respective homes. Scared but ready to take our punishment, Nadia and I sprinted all the way back.

When I saw three police cars with blinking lights parked in front of my building, I wondered if anybody was burglarized or if someone had been hurt. Onlookers assembled along the sidewalk and some of our neighbors were grouped around our lobby. But I was in too much of a hurry to even worry about anything except reaching my apart-ment. I pushed past everyone. After all, I had my own problems. Facing my strict mother without a rational explanation for my tardiness seemed like a phenomenal task. I wasn't even going to negotiate my punishment. Instead I intended to plead for mercy.

Counting the worn-out marble and tile steps as usual, I raced upstairs.

"Seven... sixteen... twenty-eight." I hated living on the fifth floor. "Thirty-five... fifty-two..." At step number sixty-two, a cold draft sailing through the busted window pane on the final landing made me shiver. "Seventy-three, that's the end!" I panted, out of breath.

Instead of pressing the buzzer, I turned the knob. Sometimes folks forgot to lock up. When the door opened, I was elated by my good luck. Warily, I snuck inside and entered the small foyer. Strange muffled voices echoed from the other end of our apartment and mingled with Buster's barking and whining.

Keeping well out of sight, I peered cautiously down the dimly lit, long hallway. Several tall dark silhouettes blocked the entrance to my mother's bedroom. I heard her scolding Buster to be quiet. A sense of foreboding terrified me. I froze when the muffled echoes were interrupted by a tall figure coming my way. I dashed inside the empty living room just off the foyer and crouched behind an armchair.

I listened while someone checked the front door and stepped briefly into the living room before retreating. After a few moments I managed, in spite of my apprehension, to gather enough courage to tiptoe down the extended hallway toward my mother. The tall men wore dark coats and wide-brimmed hats.

"It's just another kid."

"What's your name, little girl?"

Too frightened to speak, I jostled past them into my mother's bedroom. Her large brown eyes stared back with terror. Her dark pupils seemed twice their normal size and appeared to want to leap out of their sockets and shield me. My mother's long black hair cascaded over her shoulders and breasts, reaching the handcuffs that imprisoned her wrists. She shook her head at me and frowned. I easily rec-

ognized her signals, which consistently meant I
should stay out of the way, be still and quiet. My
mother was in her bathrobe and slippers and
requested permission to put on clothes and fix her
hair. They refused. When the detectives questioned
her about me, my mother responded by insisting
that she be allowed to put on appropriate clothes.

I slipped in between the space behind the partially opened door and the large bureau. From that
vantage point, half hidden, I waited and watched.
Buster's muted barks and yelps meant he was tied
up in another room.

They kept interrogating my mother, but she
persisted with her request. Finally, the detectives
acquiesced. She was permitted to put on street
clothes.

In Spanish, she instructed me to take my little
brother into one of the bedrooms and lock the door.
We were to answer no questions and speak to no
one. She told me to do the best I could until she
returned. Then she gave me God's blessing and
urged me to hurry.

My little brother Tito was hiding under the
kitchen table. He jumped with joy when he saw me.
We locked ourselves inside the only bedroom with
an interior bolt, then crept under the bed. Huddled
in silence, we listened for sounds, but the apartment remained quiet.

"Patty, tell me a story," Tito whispered.

As I tried to think of something amusing, we
heard a loud banging and blaring voices demand-

ing that we open up. Paralyzed with fear, neither one of us could budge. A tremendous blast smashed the door wide open. Numerous pairs of enormous feet wearing black shoes appeared in front of our bed. For an instant someone lifted the edge of the bedspread and a large pink fleshy face peered back at us.

"Couple of kids... scared to death."

"There's nothing in here."

"Let's go!"

A few minutes later, I trembled with panic when I heard cannons exploding. But soon I realized that the crashing sounds had been the detectives' footsteps charging down our passageway as they exited.

Tito and I eased our hold on each other and slid out from under the bed. As I stood, a chill saturated my legs; they were soaking wet and the smell of urine filled the room.

I ran to find my mother, but she was gone. Where was everybody? My older brother Joey and my Aunt Juanita? I found my great aunt in her room. She sat on her bed praying with her eyes closed, clasping a framed holy picture of Saint Lazarus against her bosom. The old woman was deaf, so I tapped her shoulder and in a calculatedly loud voice explained what had just happened.

My great aunt leaped up and began to shout in Spanish, "I know! I know! It's because of your wicked brother Manuel and his drugs. He brought those evil drug addicts and criminals into this honorable home. Patricia, I warned her, but she wouldn't listen! Your mother let the devil in and now she must pay. All of us are going to suffer!"

Frantically, Aunt Juanita undid her hairpins and loosened her long gray hair that fell below her waist. Then, deliberately and forcefully, she began yanking large fistfuls of hair out of her scalp. Opening her thin lips, Aunt Juanita bared her toothless gums and vented rasping noises followed by long loud shrieks.

She pushed me away when I tried to reason with her, then ripped at her clothes and tore open her blouse. With each loud wail, Aunt Juanita became more and more hysterical. I watched afraid to approach her, feeling utterly helpless. Then I recalled how she had behaved in the same way two years earlier at our cousin's wake, and I did exactly as my mother had done. I took a firm stance and with all the force I could muster, hoisted my right hand and slapped my great aunt as hard as I could. Immediately Aunt Juanita stopped and looked horrified at me.

"Shhh... shhh!" I brought my finger to my lips and motioned her to be quiet. "The police will come and take us all to jail if they hear you!"

Repeatedly I threatened her to be silent. Submissively, Aunt Juanita sat on her bed and began to rock and compulsively chew at her gums. Wisps of gray hair floated about, framing her wet wrinkled face. Insensible to the silvery strands of hair that had worked themselves into her toothless mouth, she continued smacking and chomping her lips.

I shut her bedroom door and checked every nook and corner of our apartment. No one was about. I untied Buster, who jumped, wagged his tail and licked my hand in simple gratitude at being free again. In the kitchen, Tito and I sat at the table and ate in silence. I glanced over at my little brother and wondered if we should go to school tomorrow. Tito probably wouldn't mind, but I was supposed to take an important spelling test.

❖ ❖ ❖

Earlier that same evening, Joey had seen the patrol cars and was told that the police were hunting for our brother Manny. Knowing they would question him, Joey opted to spend the night at our cousins' house. He returned home the next day just as distraught and confused as the rest of us.

Joey told me he was sorry he was only fourteen. "As soon as I get to be sixteen, I'm splitting from here and joining the Navy. I don't like school, like you, Patty. And, I'm tired of hanging out here, too." Joey cautioned that we all had better stay locked indoors. "If the police get us before Mama comes home, they might send us away to a reformatory."

None of us went to school the next day, or the next and the next. Either Joey or I stepped out briefly, only to purchase groceries. Aunt Juanita cooked, did housework, and the rest of the time she spent praying. Joey, Tito and I watched T.V. and sometimes I'd read them stories out loud. Once, our cousins came and said we were welcomed to stay with them. But we were sitting tight, confident that when our mother returned, life would be normal again. Mostly we waited and worried.

Finally, a week after her arrest, my mother came home, but she was never the same again. Her despondency lingered. Although there were intervals when my mother seemed more cheerful than usual, eventually her depression became chronic.

She had always prided herself on being a moral person who insisted on keeping all of our family business private. None of us were allowed to discuss family affairs outside of our home. It was after my dad died, when she couldn't provide for her children, that my mother had finally applied for public assistance. Whenever she could, my mother found piecework at the local sweat shops and sent the social workers packing from our home. Folks used to gossip about my mom and say that she was always impeccably dressed—"even when she went grocery shopping," they'd whisper. A few resented the fact that she never sat on the stoop or hung out with the other neighbors. But most others didn't mind that she kept to herself. I'd sometimes hear their favorable comments: "She doesn't bother with petty gossip because she's a person of great dignity." Those words used to make me feel proud. My mom was my role model, and for all us children she was our pillar of strength. Of course, all that was before the raid.

After the drug bust, our contentious neighbors whispered that it served her right for acting so superior. Most folks on our street forbade their children to come near us. Their kids mocked us and yelled "jailbirds" and "druggies." When we complained, my mother said we shouldn't really blame them; after all, our family had succumbed to corruption. If we could afford to move, we'd live in another neighborhood, my mother imagined, where nobody knew us and we could start over. But of course there was no money and a new environment was out of our reach. Consequently, we had to tolerate our community's rancor.

Although I dared say nothing, deep inside I knew who was really at fault. And I wished he wasn't my brother, that I had never known him. I wished Manny would die.

❖ ❖ ❖

My handsome brother Manny surfaced like a young champion when he returned to tempt us with easy prizes. Three years beforehand he had quit high school and had practically disappeared, barely keeping in touch. When he came back home, my mother was overjoyed. As Manny presented his lies with skill and cunning, she heeded his every word.

Perhaps she even wanted to believe him when he swore that the drugs he sold were not really terrible. These were recreational, sometimes medicinal, like alcohol, he insisted. People were going to buy them anyway, so why not from him?

Manny needed a place from which to deal his goods. He lived in a furnished room downtown, he explained, too small and not the right location. All she had to do, he begged, was lend him our apartment a few hours a week. He swore that he was saving enough money to open up his own business. He and his partner Sal were planning to set up a legitimate business, a laundromat, or a dry cleaners. Manny convinced her that his present situation was an opportunity for him to save money and achieve a positive future. He was counting on her help. For a few hours rental a week, he and Sal proposed more money than we could all earn in a month's time.

Back in the early 1950s, drugs were not yet a way of life in poor urban neighborhoods. The narcotics plague that was to devastate the barrios, ghettos and working-class neighborhoods throughout the nation was in its infancy.

My mother understood little or nothing about such things as drugs, so she told him that this arrangement was to be temporary. There were still young children in the house, and she wanted no conflict with the law.

At first they sold them to a few people and only twice a week: little wax bags containing an innocuous-looking white powder. But soon more people came to our door and selling heroin out of our home developed into a five day a week enterprise.

Women and men of all ages, from the palest Caucasian, Asians and Latinos, to the darkest of African ancestry, arrived with cash in hand. Some wore splendid clothes, others were shabby and unwashed. In time I learned to recognize them by the terror fixed in their eyes when they bought their packets of heroin.

The very first time Manny and Sal drove me to their studio apartment in their splendid Cadillac, I witnessed how these desperate people used the white powder. Sal left and the two of us were alone in the apartment. Manny asked me if I wanted to make a dollar. Eagerly, I said yes and followed him to the bathroom. He pulled down the toilet seat lid and sat.

"Just do as I say, and you'll earn your money."

I watched as he poured a tiny amount of water in a bottle cap then handed it to me. Manny instructed me to hold a lit match under the cap until the water began to bubble. Deftly, he mixed in some heroin and filled a syringe with the foaming white liquid. He had wrapped a tourniquet around his arm, pinpointed a throbbing blue vein and injected himself. Instantly, Manny flipped back his head and blinked so rapidly that I was sure he was having a seizure.

"Manny," I whimpered, "please don't die!" At once he sat up and smiled contentedly, thanked me and placed a dollar bill in my hand. He warned me not to tell his partner.

"Sal doesn't like me to feel wonderful." He winked and smiled. "That's because he's jealous. Now, don't be asking no questions. And, Patty, don't be telling Mama, or anyone else. OK? It's our secret."

Sal returned carrying three cake boxes. They removed two chocolate layer cakes and a coffee ring. Manny brought out a leather suitcase and emptied packs of paper currency tied with string, rubber bands and tape. They placed the money inside the boxes and resealed them.

Before leaving, we ate as much chocolate cake as we wanted.

"We'll drive uptown with my sister in the front seat... nobody's gonna stop us with a kid in the car."

We arrived in Riverdale and parked in the driveway of a stately two-story brick house encircled by tall metal gates. Manny and I waited in the car while Sal took the cake boxes inside. On our way back home, Sal gave me fifty cents and told me I was a good girl.

Afterwards, I'd wonder why inserting a painful needle with that bubbling liquid in one's arm should be wonderful or fun. What sort of magic was contained in this white powder? I mulled over such thoughts each time I watched Manny take a fix. After a few more such visits, I found excuses not to go and learned to avoid these excursions. When my mother asked if anything was wrong, I kept silent and never told about where I had been. After all, I had been trained not to reveal "family secrets."

If my mother had second thoughts concerning Manny's offer, these reservations were brushed aside. The money supplied merely for the use of our apartment transformed our lives. For the first time since our father's death, survival was no longer a struggle. We didn't have to account for every penny spent. Overnight, we could afford to purchase new winter coats and shoes. Our refrigerator was always full. We owned a new toaster-oven, washing machine and a large television set. And so the weeks passed until, quite naturally, Manny's arrangement became permanent.

❖ ❖ ❖

Eight months of relative prosperity came to an abrupt end when the FBI busted Manny and Sal, and my mother was apprehended. A few months subsequent to her arrest, the state's case against her was dismissed because of insufficient evidence.

When my mother was diagnosed with cancer a year after litigation was terminated, penitence helped her to justify her illness. Although she preferred that we all pretend those eight months of prosperity, the drugs and the arrests had never transpired, my mother had become convinced that her illness was God's punishment.

She underwent two years of a long, painful illness. Yet in all of that time we never spoke about the drugs in our home. All she ever said in her own defense was that for most of her life she'd been honest and had done her best to raise a good family. Only once had I dared question her about that week when she was locked up in jail. That topic, she warned me, was prohibited. And, it was never spoken about even among ourselves. Since then, neither Joey, Tito nor I had ever uttered a word about that ordeal.

In her final prayers she petitioned for forgiveness and implored most vehemently that her sins not be vested on her children.

At my mother's funeral, her children, relatives and friends mourned her passing. Only my oldest brother Manny was missing, because he was serving ten years in federal prison for narcotics trafficking.

After serving seven years of his prison sentence, an assortment of menial jobs barely yielded Manny a living. Periodically, Joey would call to say that Manny had been apprehended for a drug-related infraction. He would ask me to help out with a portion of the fine or bail money. Reluctantly, I always complied

❖ ❖ ❖

I only saw Manny when he attended the customary family functions, such as weddings, baptisms or funerals. None of his relationships succeeded, and he was always with a different woman. I had begun to despise Manny when I was about twelve, and in the years that followed my animosity worsened until eventually his presence made me uncomfortable. Even during family gatherings I consistently avoided interactions with him and kept my distance.

There were long periods when I didn't see Manny and heard only scant news about his life. Six months ago, after a five-year interim, Joey telephoned me. Drug abuse and alcohol had taken it's toll and Manny had become a victim of incurable cancer. A few days ago he had died.

Earlier this morning I had watched unable to grieve as his casket was lowered into the same grave where my parents and Aunt Juanita are buried.

"That's it. All four plots in this grave are full," declared Joey. "There's no room left for anybody else."

"Great, because I sure as hell have no desire to join them," quipped Tito. Everyone laughed, relieved by Tito's sense of humor.

Later, when it was just the three of us sitting in a local diner having coffee, I summoned up enough boldness to speak about our family secrets. I told my brothers all that I remembered and asked them to share their memories.

"The reason I'm asking is that I want to know if I'm actually remembering things the way they really were. Because I still blame Manny for Mama's sickness, even her death. Please, I need to know you guys remember it that way, too. And how you both feel."

An awkward silence followed. When I tried again, Tito interrupted. "Why do you want to bring up gloomy memories?" he chided. "You know, Patty, there were other people paying their respects to our brother today besides our own family. He had friends, too, you know? People loved him even if you didn't. The whole world doesn't blame Manny. In fact they don't even care about our past problems. Sure it happened. Of course we know that! Whatever he did or didn't do, our brother's dead and in his grave. Better to do like Mama wanted and put it to rest. So let's just bury that old unhappy history, too. That's what I say. Right, Joey?"

"For me, it's already buried and forgot, and I don't intend to remember. Anyway, we all grew up good, didn't we? None of us got into serious trouble. And, you done very well for yourself, too, Patty."

I could see that Joey was trying to keep composed. "You're married and have a nice family. And you got a wonderful career. Why are you dredging all that shit back up? Mama's gone! Manny's gone! We can't change the past, so don't go there, Patty. Let them rest in peace, for God's sake!"

❖ ❖ ❖

After the diner, everyone went their separate ways once more and I intended to head home. My brothers might very well have made their peace, but I had not. Instead, I had chosen to drive here to the South Bronx, hoping in this way to challenge our family's silence and connect with our past.

I looked at the clock on the car's dashboard and was surprised that it was only eleven-thirty. It felt like I had been parked in front of this wretched area for days instead of for a mere half-hour.

Suddenly, I felt a rage intensify and gather inside my chest like a solid impenetrable mass swelling and pushing against my rib cage. With each breath the pain became more and more profound. Tears brought relief, and soon I was weeping uncontrollably.

"I wish you'd never been born, you son of a bitch. You selfish bastard!" I screamed. Slowly I felt my fury relenting until it finally ebbed itself out and I slipped into a state of exhaustion.

I sat reflecting upon the possibilities of what to do next. Maybe Joey and Tito are right, I thought as I dried my eyes. Perhaps I couldn't do it now or even tomorrow, but sooner or later I was bound to put blame and hatred to rest. Besides, the idea of pursuing any more recollections in the midst of this abandoned and ravished expanse was making me feel inane and slightly bizarre.

As I turned the key, ready to start the ignition, I experienced a lightheartedness, knowing that I would soon be out of here and on my way home. But before I could start up my car, I was startled by a loud rapping and saw two women and a man staring inquisitively at me. Guardedly, I rolled down my car window.

"You looking for somebody, lady?" asked a woman of about thirty-five. She stared at my red eyes and swollen face and asked, "Are you all right? We heard you screaming."

"Yes. Well, *lo que pasa* is that I used to live on *esta misma calle,* many, many years ago. In fact *aquí* is where I grew up." Quite effortlessly I combined Spanish and English words, weaving them into the Spanglish dialect of my childhood.

They smiled, acknowledging that in spite of my affluent appearance, I must be one of them. By way of welcoming me, they inquired where my building was. I pointed to the empty lot.

"My building stood there in the middle, but on *la derecha, apartamento número diez, en el* top floor. I was remembering *mi familia* and friends when I was a kid. My oldest brother passed away; he was buried *esta mañana*... I, I guess I'm mourning his death. I suppose I'm probably grieving for all the things that happened, *y cosas...*, you know, stuff we can never change."

"*Bueno, señora,* don't grieve too much," said the man, and pointed to his chest. "It's no good for your *corazón.*" I agreed he was right, then asked how long they had lived in this neighborhood.

All three told me that they had arrived at least fifteen years ago when the neighborhood still had some significant areas intact. Since then it had all gotten much worse. My building, they said, had been gutted for over a decade. After a while they became curious and wanted to know what this neighborhood had been like in the 1950's.

"You see, I know it was nice then with *muchos* buildings, *casitas* and stores everywhere."

The man said his aunt had shown him old photo albums from that era.

"That's right," I granted. "Now let me tell you about the old Prospect and Westchester *Avenidas*..." They listened fascinated as I described, in detail, the childhood neighborhood that I had brought to memory less than an hour ago. "... And there was *mucho, mucho* activity, *y mucha gente* everywhere. *Y sin embargo,* folks were neighborly because we even left *los* doors unlocked then."

"Not like today," interjected the other woman, who was exceedingly thin and probably in her early twenties. "Locks and gates ain't keeping out no junkies and *pillos* who rob our homes. *Hoy no hay respeto,* nowhere. *Tecatos* and drugs is everywhere, and they turn people into monsters. It's very dangerous around here. People kill you for a few dollars just to get a fix. All kinds of junkies be *dondequiera,* all over this place. I bet there was no *drogas* in them days. It was very *diferente,* right?"

"Drugs were just beginning to come to this neighborhood when we moved out," I told them.

"You escaped just in time," said the man. "You're a lucky lady to have missed all these *malos tiempos,* real bad times."

"But be careful, lady," warned the older of the two women. "*Aquí hay peligro,* and you shouldn't be

parqueando out here *sola y* for so long in your
brand-new shiny car. We're *buena gente, pero* with
others you might get yourself hurt." She pointed
toward the corner.

A group of about six gang members had assembled and were gesturing in our direction.

"Don't worry, I'll tell them you're from *el* F.B.I.
and that you're making a surveillance. You know,
chequeando for drugs. This way they'll be too scared
to get too close." The man chuckled, then in a sober
tone added, "But I think it's time you better leave."

We said our good-byes. I expressed how much I
had enjoyed our conversation and thanked them for
being good people. I shut my window, made sure the
doors were locked, started the motor and drove off.

At the corner, I turned to take a last look at the
barren landscape that held my family secrets. From
out of my back window I could see the gang members lurking alongside abandoned buildings as they
discreetly tracked my car. The idea that thirty
years later I could be perceived as a member of the
F.B.I. amused me so much that I burst out laughing.

Quickly I slammed my foot on the gas pedal.
This was not the place nor was there any time left
to begin contemplating the wonders of irony.

❖ ❖ ❖

Rosalina de los Rosarios

DAME TIBORS (fl. 1220 - 1245)
LOVE SONG: *Bel dous amics, ben vos puosc en ver dir.*

Fair sweet friend, I can tell you in all truth that never have I been without desire since you have been with me as my true lover, never have I been without a longing, fair, sweet friend, to see you as often as might be, never have I repented of loving you, and never, if you left me in anger, have I known joy until you came to me again.

from: Willard R. Trask, *Medieval Lyrics of Europe* (New York, 1969), p. 39.

❖ ❖ ❖

Rosalina sat on the express bus that had brought her to New York City and south, into Spanish Harlem. Her stop would be East 96th Street, the point of demarcation that separated *El Barrio* from Manhattan's affluent upper East side neighborhood. She gazed purposefully out of the bus window as they sped through the streets of Black Harlem and East Harlem. Rosalina was searching for landmarks, bodegas, bakeries, luncheonettes and small businesses that used to line the streets of *El Barrio*. The neighborhood she remembered appeared to have shrunk, as if entire areas had evaporated without leaving a trace of what once had been. High-rise commercial buildings and low-income projects replaced the brownstones, tenements and small shops. Yet, a few streets still remained intact and they helped her recall the old neighborhood, the Spanish Harlem that she had first seen when she came from Puerto Rico. She was only eighteen then and still a *señorita*.

Her mother, Doña Petra, was a widow who suffered from chronic asthma. Her father had died when Rosalina was two and her older sister, Ana Luisa, was ten. For the next ten years Doña Petra managed to work as a seamstress. In time, her asthma worsened and illness prevented her from keeping a full-time job. Soon, even part-time work was out of the question. The doctors declared Doña Petra an invalid and she was confined at home. As the youngest daughter, it was expected that Rosalina be responsible for her mother's well-being. Except for having to attend school, coping with Doña Petra's needs became Rosalina's primary duty. That was when Rosalina had just turned twelve and entered her adolescence. It was also when she decided to become a nun.

Reciting prayers and communing with God had always been a natural inclination for Rosalina. "Why, as a young child of nine, her novenas were remarkable," her mother often boasted. "Even back then my Rosalina was able to help bereaved families." The nuns and the priest back home had taken little Rosalina aside and informed her that she had a sacred calling. "It's a divine talent," they acknowledged, and recommended that she begin to lead novenas.

In time, she became popular and people requested her services. Many said Rosalina had a voice like an angel who spoke words of comfort to the bereaved. She was soon in demand. *"Rezadoras* never charge a fee for God's work," she told her clients. "Give what you can only if you can afford it." People showed their gratitude by compensating her generously.

Although the money was welcomed, her mother's illness took first priority. There was little time for anything else. And, Rosalina's dreams of working for the Church as a sister of mercy and serving God were no longer an option. Doña Petra had no one who could support them, and after their savings were exhausted, she and Rosalina became financially dependent on her married daughter, Ana Luisa.

"Manuel and I can't support two households," Ana Luisa had written her mother. "You'll both have to come and live with us in New York City."

Rosalina and Doña Petra had left their town of Cayey, in the central highlands of Puerto Rico, in late February. It was the dead of winter when they arrived in New York City, and Rosalina remembered how the wind easily penetrated her lightweight jacket and chilled her right to the marrow in her bones.

"Mami, qué frío horrible..." Rosalina had complained of the cold, shivering as she looked up at the tall concrete skyscrapers and brick buildings that blocked out most of the dull gray sky.

She climbed up the three flights of the old tenement building, following her mother, who stopped at every third step in order to catch her breath. The small apartment that she and her mother were going to share with Ana Luisa and her husband Manuel consisted of four puny rooms. Rosalina felt like she was being confined to a prison.

"¿Pero aquí no hay balcón?" she had asked. "No. But, there's what they call a fire escape," Ana Luisa told her. "It's a kind of New York balcony... popular in *El Barrio.*" Everyone had laughed. "You'll get used to it," Manuel assured her, "everybody does eventually." Manuel had been living in New York for the past five years and spoke with authority.

During those primary weeks Rosalina missed the warmth of her native island, the familiarity of her hometown and the surrounding countryside. Each night she cried and longed to go back. That summer Rosalina spent every week waiting with desperate anticipation for Sunday. Every Sunday the family packed a lunch and picnicked in Central Park, just a few blocks west of 104th where they lived. Sitting on the grassy open knoll, Rosalina brought back vivid images of the glorious mountains that encircled Cayey. She could almost smell the moist earth and the pungent fragrance of the wild flowers that swept across the bluffs in patches of vivid colors.

But after a few months went by, Rosalina got used to living in New York City just as Manuel had predicted. What she enjoyed most was her personal freedom. Here, Rosalina went out by herself without a chaperon. New York was a huge city filled with people who didn't know each other. Back home in Cayey, the townspeople used to watch her every move and gossip behind her back. Like the time she was seen talking to Pablo Arroyo, an old classmate who had recently married. "How dare you stand right in the town square laughing and joking with a married man! You must want people to think you're *una cualquiera,* someone without morals!" her mother rebuked her, then forbade her to go to the market alone.

Rosalina managed to get part-time work as a *rezadora.* Because of her talents, people often called upon her to lead the rosaries. Except for the streets in *El Barrio,* where she lived and was recognized as an outstanding *rezadora,* Rosalina was anonymous elsewhere in the city. And it felt quite marvelous. Rosalina would often save her bus fare by walking to her destination: the large department stores on

34th Street or the Spanish Catholic church, La
Milagrosa, on 14th Street, or just about anyplace
where she might be allowed to go by herself.

Sometimes she was overwhelmed by all there
was to see, but she was never bored. There were
fleeting moments when she wanted to leave, run
away, disappear and never go back to the apartment. But, images of her sick mother, whose well-
being depended on her care and love, left Rosalina
full of shame and remorse, and she quickly put such
thoughts out of her mind.

This exquisite freedom to explore independently
lasted less than one year. Several months after her
nineteenth birthday, Rosalina became engaged to
José Luis Nieves, the man her mother had chosen
for her to marry. He had no family in the United
States, was twelve years older than Rosalina, hard-
working and reliable. "José Luis has a good steady
job, doesn't drink, and he doesn't gamble or chase
skirts. He'll come home every night," said her mother, "and never raise a hand to you if you don't give
him cause. That's what we need, someone to take
care of us. We can't continue living on your sister's
charity and in such crowded quarters."

When she turned twenty, Rosalina married José
Luis Nieves. Everyone agreed that her mother had
made a good match for her daughter. All three, Rosalina, her mother and José Luis, moved into a larger and more comfortable apartment. José Luis was
just as her mother had predicted, good, hardwork-
ing and loyal. Except for a game of dominoes and a

few beers every Friday evening with his friends, José Luis possessed no bad habits.

Theirs was a match of convenience, and Rosalina's training from early on to be obedient and never to make demands made for a marriage without conflict. Therefore, as long as her extra work as a *rezadora* didn't interfere with her duties at home, Rosalina was allowed to continue her calling.

As her reputation grew, even Father Pedrazo, of St. Cecilia's on 106th Street, became aware of Rosalina's praying skills. He recommended her to members of his parish as a first-class *rezadora*. Eventually, Rosalina built up a following and became well-known as *Rosalina de los Rosarios*. The extra money she earned in tips was welcomed by her family. But for Rosalina it was the work itself that had value.

For the next ten years Rosalina continued to live in this way, year after year, until quite unexpectedly she met Daniel. She remembered that day vividly when she had accepted the gift of passion and how it had changed her life.

❖❖❖

Rosalina felt someone poking her shoulder and was startled by the loud honking of the bus.

"Wake up, lady, or you'll miss your stop!" shouted the man sitting beside her. "Hurry up!" She had forgotten that she was still on the bus. "All right. Thank you."

"This is your stop, lady!" the bus driver announced, and opened the doors. "Nap time's over. Let's go!"

She forced herself up and out of her seat and stepped off the bus. The cold wind lashed out and Rosalina shivered as she headed east at 96th Street and proceeded north across the border into *El Barrio*. As she reached the corner of Lexington Avenue and 100th Street, a blast of frigid air lashed out without mercy and she lost her footing. Quickly Rosalina grabbed on to the metal post of a street sign, escaping a nasty fall, and caught her breath once more. She spotted a bodega just a few yards further on and rushed inside. The strong smell of Spanish coffee made her feel welcome, and she ordered a cup.

"To go?" asked the proprietor. "To drink here with milk and one sugar," she responded. Rosalina smiled, suppressing a chuckle. Here she was, arriving in *El Barrio* for the second time and it had to be in February. Standing close to the hissing radiator, Rosalina took off her gloves and rubbed her stiff fingers, numbed by the cold, until she felt the warmth return to her hands.

The bodega was poorly stocked with several shelves of basic canned goods and boxed items. Over to the side near a dilapidated freezer two wooden bins held some bruised plantains, assorted tubers and a few wilted tomatoes and cucumbers. When several customers came in and placed their bets on the numbers, Rosalina realized that illegal betting was how the owner made his living.

Rosalina felt her body relax as she sipped the hot coffee and enjoyed the warmth. "It's that time of year," she said, "when the wind is like a monster and the cold weather hurts."

"Be careful," warned one of the customers, a short portly man. "My neighbor, an elderly lady, fell this morning and broke her hip. We had to take her to the hospital."

"It's the ice on the ground that's really dangerous," said the proprietor. "That's why I always make sure the front of my store is clear and salted over. I don't need no lawsuits."

"But you got insurance for that, don't you?" asked a woman, probably the short man's wife.

"Yeah, but that only covers a certain percentage... and if they want, people can find a crooked doctor to say they got badly hurt. And even worse, they can sue and take away my business..."

Rosalina listened as they spoke about the weather, accidents and ailments. Standing here drinking her coffee, it did not seem possible that she had been gone for twenty years. Yet this was so because she was standing among strangers. Rosalina knew no one that lived in *El Barrio* anymore. Relatives or friends had either died or moved out. It was hard to believe that only yesterday she had received that telephone call summoning her to pray.

There had been a time when she received many phone calls and when her professional reputation was held in high regard. Folks remarked that her recitation of the rosaries and especially her litanies could be matched by no other *rezadora*, anywhere. Rosalina believed it was during her litanies that God spoke to her and gave her the wisdom to console the families of the deceased. She would stimulate the mourners to release their anguish, and help them accept death as fated by God.

"Dead souls are destined to exit this earth and seek their place in the spiritual world," she instructed her clients. "Let them travel in peace. Your physical attachments will create confusion. Spirits cannot depart this world in peace if the living refuse to accept death."

Most people agreed that Rosalina de los Rosarios was the best, and so she was never without work. But that was two decades ago, before she had left *El Barrio*.

A week after Rosalina and José Luis celebrated their thirtieth wedding anniversary, Doña Petra became gravely ill and died in the hospital. It was then when José Luis decided to accept the promotion offered him as chief foreman. "The pay's real good. I'll work a few more years until I retire. With our savings and my pension we'll have enough money to go back to Puerto Rico and buy a house in San Sebastían where my brothers live."

The food-processing plant was located in Putnam County in upstate New York. At first Rosalina became upset because they were moving so far from everyone she knew. But José Luis had insisted, and reminded her that Ana Luisa and Manuel had moved to California years earlier. There was no one else holding Rosalina in *El Barrio*. Finally she agreed. They relocated to a small suburban community near the plant and bought a one-bedroom condominium with a terrace. "It took thirty years," José Luis joked, "but you got your *balcón*. You got to admit it beats a fire escape."

Three years later, José Luis, who had never been ill or missed one day of work, suddenly dropped dead of a heart attack. Rosalina had not expected to be left a widow. Once, early in their marriage, when she was struggling with a severe bout of pneumonia, José Luis had stayed by her bedside and pleaded, "Don't leave me. Promise me we'll grow old together. Rosalina, don't leave me alone. Promise..." She could barely speak, but she had nodded her head and whispered her promise.

After José Luis died, she thought of going back to Puerto Rico, or even returning to *El Barrio*. Yet the idea of leaving her quiet life did not appeal to her. In the past three years Rosalina had grown used to the peaceful atmosphere and the safe streets of her suburban community. She had made a few friends, attended church, and worked as a volunteer in the local hospital. Besides, she barely knew José Luis' brothers in Puerto Rico and had no family of her own there anymore. The apartment was all paid for, and José Luis had left her a generous pension and ample savings. Finally, she decided there was really no point in moving and decided to stay put. Yes, Rosalina had told herself often enough during the years that followed, José Luis was a good provider. Mami was right about that.

"One more cup?" asked the proprietor. Unaware and deep in recollection Rosalina didn't hear him. "Hey, lady! Another cup?" he repeated. "You look like you're in another world, lady. You must have serious stuff on your mind. Have more coffee. There's no charge."

"No, thank you." Rosalina blushed embarrassed at being caught reminiscing. She checked her watch. "It's just that I have to visit someone. I don't want to be late. Besides, it gets dark out early at this time of year."

She had promised the family that for the next nine days she would commute to *El Barrio*. They in turn promised to pay for her transportation and make sure she got on the express bus for a safe return home each night. Now, she wondered if she hadn't been a bit hasty considering the terrible winter weather. She certainly hadn't come out here for the money. Rosalina smiled, knowing in her heart that the opportunity to commit to her calling once again had been too tempting to resist.

Her last recitation had been ten years ago for a family whose mother had passed away. Since that time, Rosalina had not performed as a *rezadora*. That family had lived in Jamaica, Queens. For a full nine days and until the novena was completed, they had dutifully driven her back and forth from Jamaica to her home. Rosalina followed the custom and never asked for a fee. When she remembered her large tip, Rosalina beamed, knowing they had been satisfied with her work.

Yet, perhaps because the commuting was too troublesome, she had not been called again. Once she had moved out of *El Barrio* things began to slack off. When José Luis was alive she still had a request now and then because he could drive her back and forth from *El Barrio*. But once he was gone, the calls stopped. After all, Rosalina reasoned, she didn't drive, didn't have many friends and was reserved by nature. She was not one to chase after people.

But she couldn't blame it all on a change of neighborhood and an environment where there were few if any Latinos. Today everyone abandoned tradition, not just her own people. Nowadays, it was usually the priest who said the final prayers at the funeral chapel the night before burial, to be followed by morning mass the next day. The dead were put to rest without the nine days of prayers that should follow. Not too surprising for Rosalina, who had witnessed many changes in her lifetime.

It was past sunset and outside darkness spread throughout *El Barrio*. The freezing wind stung her eyes making them tear and numbed her nostrils making it painful to breathe. Rosalina stepped inside a doorway, wiped her eyes then blew her nose. She calculated that she still had to walk several streets uptown and then cross over toward Third Avenue. Rosalina was a great one for walking, and prided herself on her agility. But tonight in the dark and bitter cold streets, she felt her age. Her left shoulder was beginning to ache from bursitis and the arthritis in her right knee was making it painful to walk. She knew she'd have to rest several times before she reached her destination.

After struggling with the cold, and suffering with the pain and stiffness in her joints for another three blocks, Rosalina found refuge inside the frame of another doorway. There she protected herself from the fierce cold and patiently waited for her rapid breathing to subside. Slowly she wiggled her fingers and toes until the numbness receded and some warmth returned to her limbs.

The high street lamps illuminated the empty street. No one in their right mind would be out on a night like this, thought Rosalina, even the muggers are staying home this evening... Well, thank God for small favors. But, she wondered how she would manage another eight nights. Someone will have to pick me up at the bus stop next time, she decided, or I won't make it.

In spite of her discomfort and pain, the familiar surroundings brought back memories that excited her. It was as if the stoops, doorways, alleys and empty lots all held a piece of her personal history. With each memory there was Daniel, always he was there. Daniel had made her marriage of thirty years to José Luis bearable.

They had been lovers for twenty of those years.

Rosalina heard her own laughter when she remembered Daniel's sweetness and their passion, never ending, always urgent. "It's enough to still this wind," she whispered, and, giggling like a young girl, forgot about the pain in her right knee.

Rosalina reached the public school on the corner and leaned against the receding brick wall that blocked the wind. Daniel was a good family man with four kids. "Linda, Susanna, Danny and Hector." She recited their names and remembered how in the afternoons she'd come to watch them play right here in this schoolyard. Her own marriage had been childless. At first José Luis, her mother and everyone had assumed Rosalina was barren, until the doctors informed them differently. A childhood disease, possibly mumps, had made José Luis sterile and his condition was irreversible.

Whenever she approached him about adopting a child, his answer was always the same. "I only work for what's mine, not to support what another man had a good time making." José Luis was laconic and reserved by nature. Early in their marriage he had made it clear to Rosalina that his home life had to be carefully organized to meet his needs exclusively. When he came home from work, he drank only one light beer, ate supper, read the paper, watched television and went to bed before nine. Because José Luis was not mean or abusive to Rosalina, she could never decide whether José Luis was unwilling or in fact incapable of sharing his emotional life.

José Luis never displayed intentional cruelty during lovemaking. He simply craved only his own sexual release. When he wanted sex, he took Rosalina without hesitation, achieved satisfaction and turned away, dismissing any further intimacy.

After being married for ten years she met Daniel when he attended one of her recitations. It was a novena for the tragic death of a young mother who had left four very young children orphaned. On the first night of the novena neighbors and friends squeezed into the living room. Rosalina knelt and prayed before the altar that held a photograph of the deceased, fresh flowers, a jar of holy water and lighted candles alongside a crucifix.

"... and you will be resurrected to immortality resting gently upon the wings of the angels..." Those who knelt behind her answered with appropriate responses, "... pray for us sinners, Mother of God..." After her prayers, Rosalina stood and turned to face those in attendance. Everyone listened attentively while she proceeded with her litanies.

"God in heaven, why did You take her? Why, when she still has four babies to raise and a husband who needs her care and her love. Is this an act of cruelty? To punish the living? Surely, Mariana was a wonderful person... tell us, tell us Mary, Mother of God, blessed in thy womb by your son Jesus, why take her?"

Daniel watched, mesmerized by Rosalina. Her thick brown hair fell in soft waves and delicate curls framed her wide face then cascaded down below her shoulders. Her body swayed lightly from side to side. Rosalina created an aura that made her appear as if she were suspended in space. Her voice echoed through the stillness of the apartment, each word spoken with care and compassion.

"Let her go, Carlos..." she told the young widower. "You and your children will find peace among the living when you release your sorrow and permit Mariana's soul to enter the spiritual world. Give her your blessings..." Sobs and cries were heard from members of the family.

For the first time in her life, Rosalina was finding it hard to immerse herself in her litany because that man kept staring. His eyes were devouring her.

"Holy Mary, celestial queen... open your heart for Mariana. Welcome her to the kingdom of heaven..."

How could he behave like that at a time like this, she had wondered. Nonetheless, she felt totally defenseless under his gaze. Weaving in and out of the Most Penitent Sorrow and other prayers, Rosalina realized that she was scarcely able to concentrate. She had become much too aware of this attractive man who appeared spellbound by her every move. Now it was he who had begun to intrigue her and it was all she could do to continue without looking in his direction.

That very night he approached her and invited her out for coffee. "Your wife isn't here, but you're married with a family," she reproached him. "Doña Elba told me."

"And, so are you married," he responded, taking her by surprise. "Please, I just want to talk to you. I think we both need a friend. But if you're afraid people will talk, let's meet downtown." He pressed a slip of paper into her hand with the name and address of a small restaurant. It was way over on the other side of Manhattan, downtown in the Chelsea area. "Please... I have to see you," Daniel pleaded, and arranged a time to meet. "Don't disappoint me."

Rosalina crumbled the small slip of paper at first, knowing that she should throw it away. Instead she held it tightly in her fist, and eventually slipped it into her pocket. All that night she thought only of this man who had stared at her shamelessly. She remembered his smile and still felt his strong hand pressing into hers. Nervous at first and ill at ease, she nonetheless managed to meet Daniel as planned. From the very first they spoke as if they were old friends, easily and intimately. When they met for the second time they made love. It was the beginning of a love affair that lasted for twenty years.

Secrecy was everything, they both agreed, since neither one wanted to disrupt their families. Rosalina and Daniel rented a small furnished room down on Horatio Street near the waterfront, and far from *El Barrio*. Their love nest served them well for almost two decades. They met once or twice each week, and whenever they could get away without arousing suspicion. They confided only in each other and took great care not to be seen. With perseverance and good luck they were never found out.

Rosalina discouraged birth control. Deep inside she longed to have Daniel's baby. After several years her wish finally came to fruition. For the first two months her joy was overwhelming. But she knew that she could not have the child. The lives of all the people they both cherished and loved most would be ruined. The shame she would bring to her sick mother and sister, Ana Luisa, not to mention José Luis as well as Daniel and his own family had made the birth of their baby impossible.

It was hard to find a reliable doctor who would rid her of the pregnancy. In those days abortion was considered a crime, and so it was dangerous and expensive. They both managed to get the money, and Daniel found a good doctor who performed the abortion safely. Rosalina became weak and was ill for two weeks afterward. Her family thought she had a mysterious malady and insisted on calling for a doctor. It was perhaps the only instance where she vehemently disobeyed them. "No! If you call a doctor I'll move out," she threatened until they finally agreed to give her more time to recover.

For a short interval after the abortion, Rosalina and Daniel fell out of love, and decided to part. Each felt betrayed by the other because neither had made an effort to keep the child as proof of their love. Rosalina even wondered if their union had been a lie.

Because she never once shared her secret love affair with anyone, Rosalina felt abandoned by Daniel. He had become her best friend and confidant. As the weeks passed, her life seemed unbearable without him and she relented. Daniel was ecstatic with the reunion; he had been just as miserable.

"Ours is not a love that's meant to have children or the respectability of marriage...," she had told him. "It's got nothing to do with that. Besides, we already have our families." In the end, they embraced and agreed that they had indeed behaved in a responsible and honorable manner.

Even now when she was far beyond her childbearing years, those memories of having once created life haunted Rosalina.

Foolishness, all this thinking about ancient history. Mama's gone, Ana Luisa, too, as well as José Luis, Rosalina told herself. Her two nieces lived in California and her nephew was in Atlanta. Her small family was scattered across this large country. "Nobody's left from the old days...," she whispered, and once more stepped briskly, confronting the frigid winds.

That man in the bodega was right. She was lucky that there was no ice on the streets, otherwise she'd give up going any further. Rosalina remembered she couldn't even telephone the family to come and get her because she had memorized their name and address, leaving their phone number at home.

As she turned the corner, she passed by the building where Daniel and his family had once lived. She couldn't begin to count the many times

she had walked by just to catch a glimpse of Daniel.
Sara, his wife, was a nervous woman and high-
strung by nature. She was nonetheless a good
mother and a decent person, always willing to help
others. Nobody could quarrel about that. Daniel
and she had agreed they were both married to good
people and that their married lives were set apart
from their passion for each other.

It had been Sara's dream to return to Puerto
Rico and live out the rest of her life there. Finally,
the time came, and days before their departure
Daniel had given Rosalina an option. "I won't go. I
can stay on in *El Barrio* and work. That's a legitimate excuse. Tell me to and I'll stay."

"I can't make that decision for you! I can't cope
with that responsibility." Rosalina had argued.
"Your children are almost all grown, so do what you
want. Please don't ask me." When he pressed her
further, wanting to know if she would leave José
Luis, she answered as she always had. "Maybe in
time, but I can't promise you. You have a family to
fall back on, but José Luis has no one, no one but
me. He mustn't grow old all alone. He's been a good
husband. He's always taken care of me and my
mother. I owe him at least that much."

That was their last argument as well as their
last time together. Later that same year she and
José Luis had also left El Barrio. Not sure whether
she had stayed married because she had promised,
or perhaps out of gratitude, Rosalina murmured,
"Maybe it was just time for the two of us to part..."

Her vivid memories of Daniel were beginning to make the reality of their long separation seem insignificant.

She trembled against the cold wind and walked up to check the corner street sign. Rosalina sighed with relief when she realized that she had finally reached 116th Street. She was amazed to see how many of the fine old brownstones had been restored. In fact, sidewalks had been repaired and the entire street had gone through a good deal of renovation.

Rosalina walked on a bit further and located the building. She put on her eyeglasses and searched for the right name. "Enrique Villegas," she whispered. The conversation had been brief. A man's voice had simply said his father-in-law had passed away. It was the family's request that a *rezadora* be called in for the novena and she had been highly recommended. Upon pressing the buzzer and announcing herself, the door lock released. Inside, a voice echoed down the stairwell, beckoning her up two flights. As was the custom, the novena always began the evening of the day after burial and everyone, friends and family, attended.

A man of about forty-five escorted her into a crowded living room and introduced his wife. "It's my dad who died," she told Rosalina. "You probably don't remember me, but you were a friend of my parents." She smiled affably. "In fact, some of the older folks here say they remember you. But, you must be frozen from the cold. Let me get you some hot chocolate."

Rosalina observed that a table of refreshments was nicely set out with the traditional coffee and tea alongside the water biscuits, white cheese and guava paste. She knew that in the kitchen they would also be serving the finest assortment of Puerto Rican rums. It had been years since she had seen this kind of display, and for an instant time had no meaning.

Several of the older people greeted her and, upon introducing themselves, refreshed her memory. Rosalina recognized a few of them as casual acquaintances with whom she once had friends in common.

Before she could ask about the person who had died, she was led to the altar. A large crucifix, along with a jar of holy water, lighted candles and freshly cut flowers in two vases, were neatly arranged on a handmade white lace cloth. Old family photographs were also on display. Rosalina again put on her glasses and saw a young Daniel smiling at her in one photo, a marriage picture of Daniel and Sara, two family portraits of them with their four children, and a photo of Daniel appearing just as she had last seen him before he left. The largest photograph, in the center of the altar, showed a much older Daniel with snow-white hair who stared out at her. She had never been able to imagine Daniel as an old man, and yet his familiar grin and the sparkle in his eyes had not changed. Self-consciously, Rosalina smoothed back her own gray hair, aware for the first time that they had both grown old.

Rosalina could hardly breathe as she scrutinized each photograph, carefully drinking in every minute detail of his image. Suddenly she felt faint, as if her legs were about cave in. Instinctively, she clutched her treasured rosary and held it against her pounding chest in an effort to gain some strength and composure.

People rushed over. "Are you all right? You look ill." The voices melted into a loud hum and her surroundings began to dissolve and she floated into darkness.

Rosalina travelled through the darkness and found herself in her lover's arms, blissfully content. They had just finished making love and he handed her the rosary beads. "You were like a goddess when I first saw you reciting the novena. Your eyes were as intense as two hot coals and your hair was as radiant as a tropical sunset. I fell in love with you right there and then. I had to give you something special to show you how I felt, so I searched until I found the only rosary beads worthy of my love goddess."

She had examined the rosary made of ivory, with each bead beautifully carved by hand. The gold cross with the body of Christ so delicately sculpted glistened in her hand. "This rosary will bind us. We'll be lovers forever," he had promised. "Just me and Rosalina, my love goddess."

From the very first time that Daniel had made love to her, Rosalina had known that they would go on savoring each other. In their cramped love nest,

three stories above the noisy New York City waterfront, their passion remained undisturbed. The
shrill clamor coming up from the loading docks,
footsteps hitting the pavement, and the traffic roar-
ing down the West Side Highway filtered up into
their private world and diminished. Nothing ever
infiltrated the intensity of their yearning. Nothing
ever disturbed their world of lovemaking. And as
the years went by, their appetite for each other only
increased.

A sharpness stung her breath and Rosalina
began to cough. When she opened her eyes she lay
on a large bed with her host eagerly standing watch
over her. "How are you?" she asked. "We gave you
some spirits of ammonia to revive you. You were so
pale, we were afraid we might have to call a doctor."

"I'm all right," said Rosalina. "It was a long trip.
Too long, I'm afraid. I doubt that I can do this job.
I'm sorry."

"Please don't worry. The important thing is that
you're all right. But, I know you knew my parents.
Remember my father, Daniel Clemente? My mother's name was Sara. I'm Linda, the oldest. My parents had moved to Puerto Rico. We thought Papi
would go first since he had been sick for many
years. But it was Mami who died just about three
years ago. Anyway, we had brought Dad back here
for treatment at Sloan Kettering Hospital. My own
kids are grown now and my husband and I thought
we'd move back to *El Barrio*. Try out living here.
After we saw how they renovated this street and

some of the surrounding area, we bought this wonderful apartment. It's in a great location near the park and the museums.

"My dad was going through chemotherapy and having a rough time. We thought he'd want to be buried back in Puerto Rico next to Mami. But he surprised us by insisting that he be buried here at St. Michael's cemetery in Long Island. Can you imagine? Papi's last request was that we have a traditional service and it was urgent that we call you. 'Find her, find *Rosalina de los Rosarios,* and let her recite the novena for me' were his exact words. We had a difficult time finding you." Linda paused. "Maybe it was foolish of me to insist that you travel in to do the novena. You're exhausted! My goodness, I'm being so rude. Would you like some tea or water? What can I get you?" Rosalina took some water.

How much she is like her mother Sara, thought Rosalina. Nervous but also kind and thoughtful. Rosalina felt her rosary beads; they were still in her hands. Daniel had wanted her to be here... to know. A burial plot, as well as a place for her name on José Luis' headstone, awaited her at St. Michael's cemetery, where she planned to be buried. Now, Daniel also awaited her.

Rosalina composed herself and managed to visit with some of the guests. She apologized for not being able to continue the full nine nights. "I'll lead you on the first night, but then you must find someone else to finish.

"Don't worry, I know a *rezadora* who lives on the lower east side," said Linda. "We'll make all the necessary arrangements."

Grasping her rosary, Rosalina knelt before the altar while the others gathered behind her, kneeling in sorrow.

"The archangel Gabriel greeted Mary and said: 'God will save you, for you are full of grace, and the Lord is with you...'"

Rosalina thoughtfully entwined her rosary in her hands and carefully stroked the delicate gold cross and each bead as she spoke

"... you have been a son, a father, a husband... you have loved, been loved in return, and revered. Now your mortal life is over. Go forward, Daniel Clemente. Go into the kingdom of heaven and there you will find peace and eternal love. You belong in the spiritual world, Daniel. No need to be afraid. Go gently and without fear. Go with the knowledge that endless love awaits you."

Rosalina refused to take any money, but accepted the car service that would take her home. As they parted, Linda embraced Rosalina. "You were wonderful," she said. "Especially when you spoke about my father's devotion to his family. His love for my mom and us kids. It was as if you really knew him. Now I can see why Papi wanted you to lead the novena. You really do remember my father Daniel. I can see that."

"Oh, yes," smiled Rosalina. "Like I said, I remember your mother Sara and you, your sister

Susanna, and your brothers, Danny and Hector." She remembered it all.

Rosalina watched from the window of the taxi as the streets of *El Barrio* rapidly slipped past her and ultimately disappeared from view. In the speeding taxi along the F.D.R. Drive, Rosalina knew that this had been her final visit to *El Barrio*. Daniel had found her and she had been called to help guide his soul into the immaterial world. There he waited. Even after death, when their mortal beings had ceased to be and their souls had entered the spiritual world, they would go on being lovers forever.

❖ ❖ ❖

Blessed Divination

For the past hour, Carmen Alvarez had remained sitting on her bed in the same position with her feet crossed at the ankles, hands holding the cablegram squarely in front of her, re-reading the news. She examined each sentence and considered every word. From time to time Carmen even read the words out loud, determined to grasp the truth of Mike's message.

Dear Carmen,
Janet and I were married last night by a justice of the peace. No big deal. Now on to a *short* honeymoon. (You know what a workaholic I am!) Carmen, I am confident you already knew it would never work out between us. This is the best way for everybody concerned. One day you'll thank me.
Mike

P.S. Hate me if you want to. But only a little.

"Shit! It's true." Suddenly Carmen heard her own words, put down the cablegram, went over to the dresser and looked at her image in the mirror. "The bastard actually did it! Me, confident? About what... being dumped? And best for who... for Mike and Janet, not for me!" She felt a tightening in her chest. "You had your cake and swallowed me whole and now you spit me out of your life like bile! THANK YOU for stealing five years of my life and ripping my soul to pieces. *¡Carajo!* You miserable motherfucker!"

Overwhelmed by feelings of total defeat, she began to whimper, and her incessant weeping escalated until breathing became painful and she trembled with rage. Each time she blinked, her swollen eyelids stung with pain.

"Son of a bitch. *¡Hijo de la gran puta que te parió!* Married! Ma warned me. She knew. You used me, Mike. *Ladrón...* thief. I want my life back and all those years back. I'm going to collect. One day you'll pay me for every minute you took from me, every second. You owe me! Mike. Michael, Mi..."

Carmen's breathing accelerated into rapid hiccups and her words diminished into gasps. Muscle spasms seized her arms and legs and her body stiffened. A pounding inside her head was followed by exploding prisms of light. Carmen started toward the doorway, but thunderbolts of bright light blinded her and she struck the wall. When she tried to shout for help, her tongue felt stiff as cardboard and she could not make a sound. Instead, she emitted convulsive gasps that ejected streams of drool. As her body hit the floor, Carmen felt the room spin and she plummeted into unconsciousness.

Concepción, who had been listening to the radio while she prepared supper, was startled by a heavy thud that shook the apartment and rushed to investigate. She found her daughter sprawled across the floor, her face and chest wet with saliva. Carmen's blouse was ripped open and the buttons strewn about the room. Concepción knelt down to examine the bloody scratches stretching across Carmen's face, arms and neck. She became terrified. It had been many years since her daughter had endured such an *ataque*.

At age ten Carmen began to suffer from self-abusive fits of temper, scratching and biting herself, and ultimately convulsing. After endless tests and examinations, the doctors told Concepción there was nothing physical that was causing the seizures. Her daughter was not an epileptic, they concluded. It was psychological. Concepción was told to seek counseling or wait for Carmen to outgrow those terrible tantrums.

Mrs. Kaplan, the school psychologist, determined that as an only child, Carmen always wanted her own way and was spoiled. Her diagnosis was that both mother and daughter should seek therapy. Concepción concluded that the last thing she would ever do is pay a total stranger to meddle into their private affairs. Instead, she took Carmen to Doña Clara, who was a well-known healer and spiritual-

ist, highly regarded in their community. Doña
Clara's reputation was impeccable because her
clientele swore that her healing and treatments
accomplished miracles.

After meticulously anointing Carmen with oils
and herbs and praying over her, Doña Clara
entered into a trance. When Doña Clara regained
consciousness, she took Concepción aside and pronounced her diagnosis.

"Sometime in a past life, perhaps many incarna-
tions ago—it's difficult to get at all the exact details
because wandering souls can be incredibly resis-
tant—" Doña Clara explained, "Carmen was mur-
dered as an infant by her mother, who then took
her own life. The infant was never baptized and
died with the original sin. Without baptism the
child's soul was never released into the spiritual
world of heaven. With each incarnation, that
infant's meandering soul gained more and more
strength.

"That child's spirit has always remained a part
of Carmen and cannot rest. It's like an angry
demon inside your daughter, driving her to seek
revenge for the heinous crimes her mother committed, you see. But Carmen's guardian angel is fighting hard to protect her by battling against the
demon. These internal confrontations are the cause
of her convulsions."

Doña Clara prepared oils and herbs and consci-
entiously gave Concepción instructions for massag-
ing Carmen's entire body with them. She also

blended a specific remedy of herbal teas to help soothe Carmen. Finally, Doña Clara gave Concepción a ritual of prayers devoted exclusively to the Blessed Mother. It was the duty of both mother and daughter to participate in this cleansing.

"The Blessed Mother will intervene and with my remedy, you will succeed in driving the demon child out of her. But you must continue the treatment until Carmen gets her period," she warned. "It's only after she becomes a woman that the demon child can be permanently expelled. Then Carmen's guardian angel will take over and continue to look after her."

Concepción carefully followed the instructions given, and as the months passed, the fits lessened. Then, exactly as Doña Clara had predicted, when Carmen got her period at age twelve, these *ataques* disappeared completely.

Concepción stared at Carmen's limp body and could hardly remember the last time her daughter had lost control. It had been over twenty-five years ago. Now, it looked very bad, very bad, indeed.

She rushed over to get her neighbor, Soledad Martínez, and together they managed to lift Carmen back onto the bed. The two women undressed Carmen, tended her wounds, then knelt and prayed to the Blessed Mother. They implored that as the Mother of Jesus, the Virgin Mary help Carmen to forget all about Mike Rosenberg.

When Carmen regained consciousness, she became profoundly depressed, whimpering that she

only wanted to die. Their doctor prescribed a seda-
tive by phone. He told Concepción it would give her
daughter a good night's sleep until he could conduct
a full examination on the following day.

After her daughter was sound asleep, Concepción showed Soledad the cablegram. "See? This
Mike was only using her. He never intended to
marry her." She grimaced in disgust. "But Carmen's
so naive, she acts like a seventeen-year-old virgin."

"We've all been stupid when it comes to men."

"But, Soledad, even now at thirty-eight, when it
comes to men, my daughter is still a *pendeja*, a poor
sucker."

"Yes, but who knows, maybe after this shock
she'll grow up." Soledad tried to comfort her friend.
"Sometimes this kind of disappointment can make a
person stronger."

Concepción said nothing to Soledad, but she
clearly remembered how the Mother of Jesus had
helped them when Carmen was a child. Concepción
sought help once again from the Blessed Mother by
pledging a novena in Carmen's name.

Soledad volunteered to light a candle to the
Sacred Heart of Jesus and devote her Sunday
prayers to Carmen. Prayer, they both agreed, was
the best solution. Faith in God and prayer would
make Carmen well and happy again.

More than once, Concepción was tempted to ask
Carmen whether she remembered her childhood
seizures, the doctors, Doña Clara and the healing.
But back then, during all the time when they were

administering Doña Clara's remedies, Concepción had never revealed to Carmen, or to anyone, what the spiritualist had told her. What could she say to Carmen now? Concepción even considered confiding in Soledad, but thought better of it. Besides, she couldn't tolerate for anyone to know their business or family history. It was nobody's concern. After all, that was a long time ago; it was not relevant now, she told herself, and kept silent.

Just about every day Concepción and Soledad prayed with Carmen. It took almost two weeks, but under Concepción's vigilant care, Carmen finally left her bed. When Carmen felt well enough to leave the house, they took her to attend Mass.

Carmen began to look forward to church. The rites of Mass brought her into a state of tranquility. She went to confession and received Holy Communion on Saturday, Sunday, weekdays, and as often as she could. Each day for the next six months, Carmen fervently prayed and faithfully continued her novenas.

At work her co-workers commented on her self-control. "She's taking being jilted pretty good," commented Rachel, one of the other secretaries. "I know I'd wanna kill the dick-head who dumped me after five years. Instead, she's praying at her desk, and during lunch she goes off to church. Carmen's changed; she's real religious now."

"If religion helps, that's good. Better that she's calm," said Rita, their supervisor, "because what's the point of fretting about what you can't change? The man's married and that's that!"

Ostensibly, religion and prayer served as her consolation. Yet there was a concealed motive driving Carmen to daily Mass and unswerving prayers; evil thoughts deluged her mind. Diabolical scenes forcibly developed in Carmen's mind, expanding into wicked apparitions. These imaginings followed her everywhere: to work, on the subway, in the shower, at night in her bed.

Fantasies of homicide and suicide ensued, one after another. It was like watching a movie on a screen in her mind. She saw her own hands soaked with the blood of her tormentors, Mike and Janet, as they gasped their last breath. Weapons drenched in blood. Blood splattered walls.

After all, she knew where Mike and Janet lived. Getting a gun would be easy. Some of her co-workers carried guns for protection. They could surely get her a handgun. With little effort she'd wait inside the lobby of Mike and Janet's building, then shoot herself right in front of them. Carmen pictured them both, remorseful and bitter with sorrow. Why had they done this to an innocent woman?

But she also wanted them to suffer. Actually, she preferred to separate and tear them apart. It would be better to shoot Janet first while Mike watched in horror. Laughing, she would blast Mike and finally herself.

Carmen wrestled between her suicide and their homicide. She alternated between outbursts of rage and moments of remorse for harboring such dreadful feelings. Fury and guilt easily consumed her waking hours. In order to rest, Carmen began to rely on sleeping pills, even for a partial night's sleep.

Church became her respite from this sinister rage. In church she could stop obsessing because, there, the images diminished. But outside of church, the fantasies never ceased. Once on the subway, a woman with eyes that resembled Janet's sat opposite her. Carmen envisioned blood spouting from the woman's eyes, flowing down her chest and body, eventually drenching everyone around her. Whenever she spied a couple strolling arm and arm, she quickly imagined Mike and Janet dropping to the ground, being ripped to pieces under a hail of bullets.

When these apparitions occurred, Carmen fled to the sanctuary of the nearest Catholic church. Once there, Carmen implored Jesus and the Blessed Mother to help her out of this dilemma. She beseeched them to bless her with clarity and deliver her from evil.

Then one evening, Carmen sat thinking in church. Except for three people sitting in the back pews, the church was empty. She reflected that she was her mother's sole support. What'll happen to Ma if I die or go to jail? If only for her, I have to go on living. As always, Carmen prayed for a divine symbol that would help her achieve a peaceful existence. Thus far, Carmen had been disappointed.

She knelt before her favorite statue of the Blessed
Mother and stared up at the Virgin's soulful eyes
and sad, graceful mouth.

"I want to accept that justice and revenge are
not for mortals but for God," murmured Carmen.
"Blessed Mother, help me, I implore you. Give me a
sign."

Suddenly, Carmen saw tears streaming down
the cheeks of the Blessed Mother.

"Carmen, Carmen...," a female's voice softly
echoed. Her name resounded from high up beyond
the vaulting and filled the quiet church. After a
moment's hush she heard a chorus chanting,

INNOCENCE SHALL BLESS YOU.
SEEK JUSTICE AND HEAVEN IS YOURS.

She trembled as the chant repeated. Each sylla-
ble pierced her skin and sent shudders through her
body.

INNOCENCE SHALL BLESS YOU.
SEEK JUSTICE AND HEAVEN IS YOURS.

Slowly the chant dwindled and all was silent.
Carmen blinked and saw that the statue of the
Blessed Mother had stopped crying. The same people sat quietly as if nothing had transpired. But
everything had changed for Carmen. She had
received a divine message for her and only for her.
Nothing would ever be the same again.

She had a mission. No longer was it just work and taking care of Concepción. Her life was now dedicated to the prophecy that had been given by the Blessed Mother herself. Only she could guide Carmen to seek out justice, and heaven, as God's blessing would be assured.

"Of course, what could be more simple and sanctified?" she whispered, and made the sign of the cross.

Carmen expressed her gratitude to the Virgin by pledging a special novena which would continue for as long as necessary, weeks, months or years, until her moment of truth arrived.

It was as if she had been healed and liberated from a perpetual affliction. Her new reality brought such welcome relief that before going to bed that night she flushed her sleeping pills down the drain.

After six interminable months, Carmen shed her fiendish cravings, her helpless misery, and embraced her future like a happy woman.

❖ ❖ ❖

FIVE YEARS LATER

"Now tell me in Spanish. Go on just like I taught you," urged Carmen. "You know how."

"*Yo te quiero mucho,*" answered Stevie in perfect Spanish without a trace of accent.

"*Sí, sí.* Yes, that's right. I love you very much. You see how Carmen teaches you and how quickly my Stevie learns. Now listen carefully... *Dame un besito.*"

She leaned forward, waiting. Obediently, Stevie stretched out his little arms and planted a kiss on her puckered lips. Carmen hugged Stevie and lifted him up in the air.

"*Mi lindo, yo te quiero mucho. Mucho mucho mucho,*" she sang as she swung him round and round playfully. Then she sat down and put Stevie on her lap.

"You are the most precious thing in Carmen's life. Do you know that?"

Stevie nodded.

"Tell me in Spanish like I taught you. *Te quiero para siempre por toda mi vida.*"

As Stevie whispered into Carmen's ear, she nodded approvingly. "That's right. You must always love Carmen, forever and forever. You must never leave and go far away. Understand?"

"Uh huh," sighed Stevie, content to be nestled in her lap as she rocked him gently.

"Remember that we are friends for life. If you ever leave and forget Carmen... why, I'll get sick and die. I'll die from missing you."

Stevie sat up and stared wide-eyed at Carmen. "Will you really die?"

"Of course, silly." Somewhat annoyed, she held him by the shoulders and stared into his eyes. "How many times have I told you that I'll die of grief."

"Then I'll never ever leave you," he vowed, holding his right hand over his heart just as Carmen had taught him. "I'll always love you and I won't go away. Honest."

"Good. Now it's time to go to sleep. Your mom and dad are coming to pick you up very early tomorrow morning."

"Let me sleep with you," he said, clinging to Carmen.

"No, you're almost five-years old. That's too old to sleep with anybody."

"Please... please," Stevie whined.

Carmen shook her head and gently ushered Stevie to the small day bed placed next to her large double bed. "Now it's time for our prayers."

Stevie knelt down beside Carmen and repeated her words.

"Jesus and the Blessed Mother, please bless my mother Janet and my father Mike. My Nana Ida, Concepción and mostly Carmen, who loves me very, very much. I will be a good boy and do as I am told. God is great and God is good. Amen."

She tucked him in, pulled the covers snugly around his small body and handed him a stuffed rabbit with half an ear missing. "Here's Panchito. He'll sleep with you and keep you company."

He shut his eyes and hugged Panchito.

Carmen stroked Stevie's hair, gently fingering the thick black curls. If Mike and Janet or Ida knew, they'd forbid him to pray. They were all non-believers. Under her guidance, Stevie had learned to believe in and fear God. Carmen had taken painstaking care to keep it all a secret. By now Stevie understood that in order for him to have God's love and protection, he should never tell.

Carmen suppressed a chuckle when she imagined how outraged Mike, Janet or Ida would be if they knew Stevie had been baptized. When he was seven months old, Carmen took Stevie to her old parish in the Bronx. Father Quiñones had become suspicious and demanded to see the baby's birth certificate. But Carmen convinced him that Stevie's parents were drug addicts who had abandoned their son. She also assured him that they were lapsed Catholics. It was a matter of extreme urgency, she insisted, because the child would soon be placed in a non-denominational foster home.

"Who knows if he will ever be baptized. He'll carry the original sin for eternity and in death be denied into the Kingdom of Heaven. Help me prevent this. Please don't fail us."

"It won't be legal," he warned, "and I can't give you papers."

"Let it be valid in the eyes of God," she perse-
vered, inflexible in her pleading, until Father
Quiñones agreed to perform a hasty but acceptable
baptism. Now, in the eyes of God Stevie was her
godchild, and they were united forever.

Carmen knew in her heart that because she
had kept her promise and prayed faithfully, the
Blessed Mother had sent Stevie to her. Just as the
voice had foretold, innocence followed. What could
be more innocent than a child, she asked herself.
Now Stevie was free of the original sin. Not only
had justice been done, but she and Stevie were
bonded by the laws of God. From now on the
Blessed Mother, through God, would lead their
way, and in time Carmen's own salvation would be
absolute.

Carmen turned off the lamp and tiptoed out of
the room, leaving the door slightly ajar. She
remembered her visit with Ida earlier this evening.
As was customary, she had taken Stevie directly
across the foyer to apartment 7B, where Ida Rosenberg lived.

"Remember, Stevie, when you say good night to
Nana Ida, don't go telling her our business," she
had warned.

Ida Rosenberg and her husband Conrad had
arrived in New York City forty-five years earlier,
during World War II. They had come as political
refugees, German Jews fleeing Europe. Ida had
been a widow for more than thirty years. Five
years earlier, she had been partially paralyzed by a

severe stroke, but her keen mind and mean temperament had not been in any way impaired. With
the aide of a cane she also managed to get around
quite successfully.

"Stevie, *mein kinder*, my little sweetheart, come
in, come in..." Ida had never lost her pronounced
German accent.

Carmen listened apprehensively while Ida, as
usual, questioned everything they had done that
day. Stevie answered Ida with simple sentences,
leaving out all the details.

They had gone to the small pond in Central
Park, where they watched toy boats being navigat-
ed by remote control. Later, Carmen had rented a
video and cuddled with Stevie to watch her favorite
Walt Disney movie, Pinocchio. Carmen had pointed
out that even though Gipetto was not Pinocchio's
flesh-and-blood father, he loved Pinocchio so much
that he turned him into a real boy. And that was
also how much Carmen loved him.

"But I am a real boy!" Stevie responded.

"Yes, but because I love you, you'll become the
very best boy!"

"Carmen, you always say that I am the best
boy."

Carmen had taken his hands and clapped them
together. "The very, very WONDERFUL best boy!"

Ida, still probing, continued to caress her grand-
son, rubbing his back gently. "Was there something
special you don't tell me?"

Stevie shook his head, "No, that's everything," he said, pleased by Carmen's smile of approval.

Later, Carmen praised Stevie. "You were a good boy and didn't tell Nana Ida nothing you weren't supposed to. You kept all our secrets. What a smart boy you are!"

Carmen had a genuine dislike for Ida. Yet she knew that it was Ida who had made it possible for her to have Stevie. Immediately after they married, Janet became pregnant. Stevie was six weeks old when Janet returned to work full-time. Mike and Janet moved into an apartment close to Ida so that during the day she could care for their infant son. Ida enabled them both to continue with their careers. But only one month later, Ida became ill.

Concepción had heard the baby's hysterical cries coming from Ida Rosenberg's apartment. After more than an hour of incessant screaming, she tried pressing the buzzer, but got no answer. Concepción called maintenance, and when they went inside, they found Ida lying on the kitchen floor, barely breathing. Concepción telephoned Carmen, who rushed home from work, eager to help.

"We were friends once," Carmen told Mike. "Let us help. Go on to the hospital and be with Ida. Ma and I will take care of the baby, don't worry." Somewhat astonished at Carmen's generosity, but grateful to receive help at a time of crisis, Mike and Janet readily agreed.

When they returned, dinner was ready, the table was set and Stevie was well taken care of, happy and secure. Carmen announced that she had already arranged to take a few days of sick leave and was prepared to care for Stevie until they had time to make other arrangements. Mike was starting his own business and Janet had just been given an important promotion. It was all too tempting and impossible to refuse.

When they offered money, Carmen was deeply offended and threatened to call off the arrangements. "We do this out of friendship, not out of greed."

"But only on a temporary basis," insisted Mike.

"We don't want to impose on you and Concepción," added Janet.

Later, they marvelled at Carmen's kindness and generosity. "I always go out with nice women," Mike joked. Janet didn't think it was funny.

Mike and Janet arranged for part-time help for Ida and hired a daytime sitter for Stevie. Carmen pitched in when sitters were not available. Weekends, Carmen encouraged Mike and Janet to leave Stevie overnight.

"Stevie's happy here with us. Get away by yourselves. Drive out to the country and enjoy your time together."

Often Mike and Janet indulged themselves by sleeping late on Sunday mornings. On occasion, they would slip away for a rustic weekend upstate. Always, Stevie remained with Carmen.

After his third birthday, Stevie went to a full-time nursery school. However, it was arranged that Carmen meet Stevie at his bus stop and take him home until his parents came by in the evening.

From the time Carmen took charge of Stevie, he had never been away from her for more than a few days. She had also given up dating or going on a proper vacation. Whenever she thought about changing her life or became tempted to flirt with a man who paid her a compliment, the chant she heard in Church would resurface and echo in her mind:

INNOCENCE SHALL BLESS YOU.
SEEK JUSTICE AND HEAVEN IS YOURS.

Immediately she would respond in prayer. "I have been blessed by Stevie. Justice is being done and heaven will surely be his and mine." Each time she heard the chant, Carmen felt sanctified.

❖ ❖ ❖

As usual, this evening Concepción sat watching television in the living room. She heard familiar sounds coming from the adjacent kitchen as her daughter fixed their drinks.

"Mami, Stevie's finally asleep. Do you want tea with cinnamon or hot cocoa tonight?" Carmen called out.

"Cocoa. Put in lots of milk; don't make it strong."

This was their nightly ritual. Mother and daughter had lived together always. They had slept in the same bed for all of Carmen's forty-four years.

"Do you know that Stevie's learning more and more Spanish every time he comes here? Imagine, and he's still only four years old. That kid catches on quick. He's so bright for his age. I tell you, Mami, when he grows up he's..."

Concepción barely listened. She was tired and bored with her daughter's raves about the boy. Stevie this and Stevie that, she mimicked, moving her lips in silence. It was all so much exaggeration. At times Concepción became concerned and even alarmed at her daughter's attachment.

"It's not just normal affection, it's an obsession with that child," she had confided to Soledad. "It's not natural. We aren't even related to Stevie."

She also knew that Ida Rosenberg had never liked her daughter. Concepción resented their obligation to look in on Ida every day and offer help. Just this week she had looked in to inquire if Ida needed anything.

"You people are always asking questions. Why are you all the time in my business? I'm not a helpless child. You cannot control me. I am not Stevie!"

"*¡Bruja malagradecía!*" she complained to Carmen. "I don't know why we have to put up with that ungrateful witch."

"We're helping Stevie's parents, that's why. They have to be happy so that I can take care of Stevie without interference."

Concepción was beyond asking her daughter what she needed with a stranger's child. By now Stevie had become the center of Carmen's life. This whole arrangement with the Rosenbergs was a source of constant aggravation for Concepción.

At night when she couldn't sleep, Concepción mulled over Carmen being so enamored of the child of the man who had so cruelly rejected her. Could she really adore the son of the woman who had been her winning rival? What logical reason could there be for Carmen's persistent devotion to Stevie? Concepción remembered all too well the words of Doña Clara, that a child's demon spirit had once possessed her daughter. Reluctantly, another apprehension would surface when Concepción wondered if Stevie was in some way linked to Doña Clara's revelations.

When those foreboding contemplations arose, Concepción prayed hard to the Blessed Mother. She implored that no harm would befall them, and that she and her daughter be safe under God's care.

These notions terrified Concepción. After all, she was all alone in this world and totally dependent on Carmen, her only living child. Concepción had once borne another child, a boy named Francisco, who was stillborn. Soon after, her husband died when Carmen had just turned five. Concepción's own parents were no longer living and her only sister had also died many years ago. Her late husband's relatives were all in Puerto Rico; they were even poorer than Concepción. She was left destitute and alone. Unskilled and with a fourth-grade education, Concepción labored in sweatshops and in canning factories, working constantly in spite of her high blood pressure. But she survived and made a home for herself and her little girl. With God's grace, she still had her daughter with her.

Carmen was her greatest treasure in life, and she thanked God for this prize every single day. Concepción would erase such foreboding thoughts from her mind. Besides, it was evident to everyone how Carmen showered Stevie with so much love. How could she possibly believe that there was anything but goodness in Carmen's affection for Stevie?

The clatter of dishes brought Concepción back to the present. These routine kitchen sounds appeased her anxiety. Ultimately, she always concluded that, after all, they were ordinary people and their lives were simply as normal as anyone else's.

"It's all just my nerves, and since I always seek protection against the evils of life through prayers, the Holy Mother will guard us," she murmured, making the sign of the cross.

Carmen poured the contents of the deep rich brown cocoa into two mugs and placed some water biscuits with slices of mild cheddar cheese and sweet guava paste on a dish. She enjoyed preparing their nighttime drinks, especially on the weekends when Stevie was tucked away and sleeping in his day bed. He had been with her the entire weekend.

"Life has it's compensations," she sighed, feeling content with her lot as she brought their tray into the living room.

In less than a month it would be Christmas. As usual, Carmen had made lots of plans for Stevie and could hardly wait for the holidays.

❖❖❖

For years now the Rosenbergs had relied upon Carmen and Concepción to help them manage a relatively smooth household. Up until recently, Mike and Janet had discussions and agreed that at times Carmen demonstrated over-possessive behavior toward Stevie. Yet they had always concluded that this was a small price to pay for the comfort and peace of mind they both enjoyed as a result of Carmen's friendship.

"When he's older and begins to make more friends, Stevie won't want all that attention," Mike assured Janet. "You'll see, it will all change."

But for a long time now Janet had been harboring deep resentment toward Carmen. Her overbearing personality grated upon Janet's nerves. She continued to be irritated at Carmen's candidness and was often offended by her excessive displays of affection, hugging and kissing Stevie, without any apparent reason. In fact, when Janet first arrived in New York, she was amazed at people's behavior.

"Everybody gets so familiar too quickly," she had confided to a co-worker. "I wasn't brought up like that."

Janet was born in rural Minnesota and had been raised as a strict Methodist. She spent most of her life in the Midwest, even finished college there. Her relationship with others had always been polite but restrained.

It was difficult for her to communicate displeasure, anger or even affection. Displaying her feelings or discussing stressful issues always made Janet uncomfortable. But lately she had gathered the courage to remind Mike that she was Stevie's mother, not Carmen. Ida agreed with Janet. Even from the beginning when Mike started dating Carmen, Ida had never liked her.

"She's too common, and no education. She reads only trashy novels," Ida complained to Mike. "Concepción only wants a good catch like you for her stupid daughter. I hope you don't get serious intentions."

But Mike had been drawn to his pretty, vivacious neighbor, who laughed at all his silly jokes and who seemed terribly impressed with his intellect. Often he'd wait by the elevator until Carmen came out of her apartment. They discovered they both had things in common; as only children they were solely responsible for their widowed mothers with whom they lived. They had both grown up in New York City, nearby on the upper West Side, and had recently moved into the building. They were also the same age.

Carmen and Mike began dating and were soon seen as a couple. Concepción didn't much like Mike or Ida. "These white people don't like Puerto Ricans. Especially the Jews, they usually marry their own kind. Be careful. That Mike doesn't want marriage. He's only using you."

But Carmen was so smitten by Mike that she dismissed her mother's warnings and ignored Ida's rudeness, trying always to be friendly. Mike continued his affair and pacified Ida by assuring her that it wasn't serious. Although he took Carmen on vacations with him and they spent many nights in hotel and motel rooms making love, Mike consistently avoided the subject of marriage. Whenever she brought up getting married, he'd smile and say that there was still plenty of time to make serious plans. All along, Carmen never doubted that someday she'd be his wife.

"The reason we haven't gotten engaged," she explained, "is because Mike's waiting to start his own business." Their romance went on in this way for four-and-a-half years until he met Janet.

Ida liked Janet immediately. She was educated and reserved. "Not like that crazy Carmen Alvarez, always talking nonsense," she told Mike. "This one is for being serious."

Although sex was no better or worse with Janet, he enjoyed the change. Janet was younger, ambitious and her low-profile temperament made

her easy to be with. Most importantly, Ida
approved. Ida was not religious, and the fact that
Janet was Christian and brought up as a Methodist
was never an obstacle. In less than six months they
were wed. When Mike and Janet married, Ida
rejoiced in her good fortune.

"Good, now we are free of that Carmen Alvarez
and her annoying mother," she had boasted more
than once. Everything had gone just the way Ida
had wanted until she had the stroke. Since that
time, and in spite of her dependency on Concepción's and Carmen's goodwill and generosity, Ida's
bitter attitude was unflinching. The old woman
barely tolerated them.

Most holidays and especially on Christmas, Carmen took care of activities while Janet usually
stayed in the background. But after giving it much
thought this Christmas, Janet decided to make her
own plans for Stevie. She told Mike she was going
to take Stevie to see Santa Claus and spend the
entire day with him.

"It's his very favorite thing to do. Anyway, it's all
been arranged at work. I'm taking Christmas week
off."

"Why now?" asked Mike, genuinely surprised.
"You never cared much about Christmas before."

"Because I am Stevie's mother. I gave birth to
him. ME! Not Carmen." Janet insisted that she was
entitled to her own day with her son. "On Christmas or at any other time if I so choose."

Mike argued that she was being oversensitive.

"It's all been arranged. Let's not talk any more about this." He recognized that tone of cool exasperation in her voice and backed off. Janet rarely made demands, but when her mind was made up, it was resolute.

❖ ❖ ❖

The Saturday before Christmas, Carmen watched Stevie as he waited his turn in line to see Santa Claus at Macy's Department Store. They had already eaten lunch at McDonald's and had done a little shopping. It was just like any other Christmas for them.

"Now I get to see Santa Claus again with Mommy," shouted Stevie when he returned.

"Yes, and you can ask Santa for more presents. What a lucky boy you are! But, remember you mustn't tell anyone. Especially Mommy, because she wanted to take you there first. This is just one more of our special secrets. Now, you must promise," warned Carmen, "like this," and crossed her heart.

"I promise," Stevie said, and crossed his heart just like Carmen.

Sunday morning, Concepción was making waffles for breakfast and thinking how she preferred these peaceful Sundays without Stevie running about. She felt too old to deal with children, although she sometimes wondered if she might feel kindlier had Stevie been her own grandchild. "I'll never know," sighed Concepción. "It's too late for that."

When Carmen answered the phone, Janet was shouting so loud that Carmen held the receiver at arm's length.

"How dare you! Just who in the hell do you think you are?" Janet's fury increased with each sentence. "Stevie's my son, Mike's my man and this is my family... damn it! I ask for one thing, one lousy event with my kid, and you deny me. You had to take him there first in order to spoil my fun. I only found out when Stevie's slip of the tongue told me he'd already had his picture taken with Santa Claus.

"You couldn't even spare me a moment of happiness with my own child. Well, it's over... all finished. You can't see Stevie anymore. YOU HEAR? I forbid it. Just keep away from him. Just stop it. Stop it! Keep away from us!"

Carmen sat motionless, the dial tone humming in her ear.

"¿*Qué pasa?* Who's screaming on the phone?" demanded Concepción. Carmen set down the receiver and explained what had just happened.

"It's just a misunderstanding, Ma. It'll be all right."

Concepción watched her daughter, who appeared much too composed. Concepción worried that perhaps her daughter was in shock. As she watched Carmen staring into space, she wanted to console her daughter, to tell her she was sorry. Yet she also felt vindicated by the confrontation, and couldn't hold back.

"I told you that one day they'd take Stevie from you. If it isn't now, it'll be the day Ida dies. They won't need us anymore and they'll move far away. Sooner or later it was bound to happen. It's time you got on with your own life!" Carmen sat motionless and unresponsive.

"And, what about me, your mother, your own flesh and blood? I count, too. We never go on a decent vacation because of that kid. Stevie this, Stevie that... I'm sick of that brat, that uppity Janet and that miserable old witch Ida and her bloodsucking monster son Mike. I'm sick of them all. *¡Basta ya! Y gracias a Dios.* Good Riddance!"

"Never mind, Ma. It's all right. It doesn't matter because it's too late. They'll never really have Stevie back. He's not theirs to take."

"What do you mean, it's too late and he's not theirs. Carmen, what are you saying?"

Carmen's smile and composure frightened Concepción. She decided to say no more. Instead, she planned to keep a wary eye on her daughter, fearing that the shock might cause her to have one of those dreadful *ataques*.

Both women proceeded with their lives as before, except they did not check in to see how Ida Rosenberg was doing and there was no talk of Stevie. Days passed, an entire week went by and still there was no communication from the Rosenbergs, not a word. Twice, without meaning to, Concepción wondered out loud and asked Carmen about what might be happening with Stevie. Each time Carmen had shrugged and said, "Don't worry about it, Ma."

Actually, Concepción's only worry was that the Rosenbergs might all come back into their lives. Things had been peaceful this past week, and she wished it would stay that way. Just the two of them, like it used to be.

❖ ❖ ❖

"I shouldn't have taken Stevie out on such a cold, wet day, especially since he had a runny nose and a cough. I should've known better," Janet said, feeling guilty about taking her son to see Santa Claus.

"Has his fever gone down any?" asked Mike. Janet shook her head.

"It's still 102, but we haven't finished the antibiotics his doctor prescribed.

Let's give the medicine a chance to work."

"It's been a week. I think we should call her. What's the big deal? You know Stevie wants to see Carmen. Her coming over wouldn't do him any harm. They're very fond of each other. After all, she's looked after him practically his entire life. I'm sure it would cheer him up, you know, lift his spirits."

"You don't get it. You just don't get it! Why don't we try for once to take responsibility for our own child?"

Janet felt as if she were fighting for her son, doing battle to win him back. She was never going to rely on Carmen again. Never. Maybe I should have done this earlier, but I'm doing it now, Janet swore, determined not be an absent mother any longer.

From the onset, when he was in bed with what just seemed a bad cold, Stevie had been asking for Carmen. Finally, Janet made him stop.

"Mommy's here now. I'll take care of you and make you all better again."

But, with each day he got sicker and now it was a full-blown case of influenza.

"The boy's sick, and we both can see he's unhappy. Let her come for a visit," argued Mike. "Besides, Carmen loves Stevie, and we owe her something for all her help. She shouldn't be excluded. After all, she's done a lot for all of us. Even for my mother."

"No, no, no! Mike, we should have done this long ago. Why do we need Carmen or Concepción always solving our problems? Ida's got us, and Stevie's got parents. They're both our responsibility. We have to stay firm on this one: he's not seeing Carmen."

"You'll use up all your sick leave," he warned.

"I don't care if I use up my entire vacation. I DON'T CARE IF I NEVER FUCKING GO BACK TO WORK!" Janet found herself screaming at Mike and swearing much too often. This whole episode was unnerving.

She paused and spoke with quiet conviction. "Stevie is mine. Carmen's not taking him from me ever again!"

Mike was tired of arguing and told her to suit herself. He left for work early and when he returned, Stevie's fever had gone up to 104.6. The doctor advised that Stevie be hospitalized in order to conduct further tests and monitor possible complications.

In the hospital, Stevie had to be put in an oxygen tank. His lungs had become badly congested. The doctors thought that perhaps Stevie had contracted a rare case of pneumonia, but Stevie's symptoms were not responding to treatment and his condition worsened with each passing day.

Janet was grief-stricken and torn up inside with guilt as she watched her son fighting for each breath. Up until now she had been unrelenting about calling Carmen. But as Stevie struggled to keep alive, Janet was gripped by fear. She panicked and felt desperate to help her son.

"Stevie, would you like to see Carmen?"

His eyes widened with interest.

"Shall I call her then?"

Quickly, he nodded.

Janet telephoned Concepción, who in turn called Carmen at work. To her surprise, Carmen barely reacted. Concepción was taken aback when Carmen arrived home at her usual time. She explained again about Stevie and said that both Janet and Mike had called several times and were waiting at the intensive-care unit. Concepción told her that she must go immediately. Carmen replied that she had no intentions of going to the hospital.

"There's no point in my going, Ma," she said calmly and with deliberation. "With the help of the Blessed Mother, I did all I was supposed to do. Stevie's in God's hands now."

In spite of her previous fears that Carmen would once again entangle their lives with the Rosenbergs, Concepción was dumfounded by her daughter's words. Yet she continued her attempt to impress upon Carmen that the boy was gravely ill.

"But Stevie might die," she argued. "He's that sick."

"I was vigilant in my faith and true to the Blessed Divination," she told Concepción. "As was fated, I have been blessed by innocence. Justice has been accomplished and heaven is our reward. My work is finished."

❖❖❖

Shortly after Stevie's death, Ida Rosenberg died. Mike was so afflicted with remorse that he was only too grateful to leave all funeral arrangements, as well as their future plans, to his wife. Janet said she would never forgive Carmen for not coming to see Stevie at the hospital or even attending his funeral.

Mike and Janet moved away without leaving a forwarding address.

After a year of dutiful grieving over Stevie's passing, Carmen shed her black mourning clothes. She did, however, give up wearing red, yellow or any bright color that might attract attention. She bought a gold locket and placed a picture of the Blessed Mother on one side and a picture of Stevie on the other side.

"He's my godchild, who is in heaven." She often explained to the other parishioners, people at work, neighbors, or to almost anyone who cared to listen, "I loved Stevie more than life itself. We were so close. It was the Blessed Mother herself who brought us together. And she knows that someday I will be with him among the angels in paradise."

Carmen showed no interest in dating. She was even more pious than before, taking Holy Communion daily. Her time was devoted to church work, and she became the chairperson of the community outreach committee. That took a good deal of her time. But now and again, she and Concepción did manage to enjoy short but very pleasant vacations.

Concepción felt very bad about the boy's death, yet she was also thankful it was just the two of them once more enjoying peaceful weekends. Their lives were back to normal. Stevie, Ida, Mike and Janet Rosenberg all now seemed to Concepción like characters in a malevolent nightmare that had ceased to exist. Her greatest consolation, however, was the fact that Carmen never again had another *ataque*.

Utopia, and
the Super Estrellas

Brenda drove her rented car toward the interior and up into the mountains, away from the seashore. Along the way we sped past roadside villages and barrios and secluded forests. Behind the lush foliage lay hidden domains where folks lived in primitive conditions with no access roads, plumbing or electricity. Dusk was turning into night and the darkness made me uneasy.

"Where is this place, how far?" I asked, hoping we weren't lost. Even the main road was a narrow thoroughfare, badly maintained.

"Don't worry, I've driven through this area before. We're heading up into the highlands and away from all the tourist places. That's why it looks so desolate. But we'll be getting there soon enough."

I had arrived two days ago to vacation in the Dominican Republic for ten days. My friend, Brenda Nieves, had rented a beach cottage for the Christmas season in the beautiful northern region outside of the resort town of Sosua. I needed to get away from the hustle and frenetic pace that living in New York required, and when Brenda invited me to

spend time there with her, I quickly consented.
Except for swimming and sunning during the daytime in our private bay and enclave of well-kept
homes and cottages facing the Atlantic Ocean, there
wasn't much to do at night. This evening, we had
opted to leave the usual assortment of tourist bars,
restaurants and local discos offered us in Sosua,
and instead enjoy some mountain music and entertainment.

After about a half-hour, we finally arrived at a
small barrio and were guided by roadside lamp-
posts and a succession of brightly lit kiosks. Brenda
steered up to a group of wooden buildings with
thatched roofs, then swung the car around sharply
and entered a roughly plowed out parking lot. I was
relieved to see other cars had already parked.

"Well, at least we aren't the only ones here," I
said, and followed Brenda around toward the front.

A red neon sign with blinking palm trees read
La Casita Disco Club. A large poster was plastered
across the entrance announcing that tonight we
were going to be entertained by GLENDA Y SUS
SUPER ESTRELLAS. ESTA NOCHE EL SHOW
AMERICANO CON LAS ESTRELLAS FAMOSAS
DE LOS ESTADOS UNIDOS — CHER, CELIA
CRUZ, ARETHA FRANKLIN, JUDY GARLAND,
DIANA ROSS Y BETTE MIDLER.

"We'll be meeting Ivan and Samuel inside,"
Brenda told me. "Ana, you'll like them. They're nice
guys. Samuel's a lawyer and Ivan is an electrical
engineer. "And," Brenda winked at me, "I might

add, they're both single, since I know you don't go out with married men. A little flirtation wouldn't hurt you. It might even lead to something. Samuel gets to New York quite often."

I smiled politely, not wanting to seem ungrateful for her efforts. But right now I wasn't interested in getting involved in flirtations, and the prospect of any kind of relationship was terrifying. Two months earlier, I had dissolved a long love affair that had been consuming and vitriolic at its worst, and ardent but oppressive during the best of times. Either way, there had been no room for moderation. Outside of our lovemaking and passion, Nick and I had disagreed and fought about most other things in life. Our worst quarrels were about female politics and my staunch support of feminism. Nick would accuse me of having no respect for men. "Your problem is that you want to be in control all the time. Instead of being satisfied to be a woman, you want to make all the decisions and act like a man!"

My rebuttal was usually about how I didn't want to be a man, and act as asinine as he did in this lifetime, or even in my next incarnation.

That's when he'd begin his verbal attacks on homosexuals. Although Nick had a few gay acquaintances, he resented the longtime close friendships I had maintained with my lesbian and gay male friends. "Maybe that's why you like being with those queers. Because you're not satisfied to be a woman. You'd rather be abnormal and hang out with sick, confused people."

Whenever Nick felt insecure about our relationship, he'd argue relentlessly, using my gay friends as the butt of his anger. "God didn't intend for two guys or two women to be in bed together. Couples are supposed to procreate. Even the Bible states this fact!" I would remind Nick that neither of us wanted children, and that he wasn't at all that religious. And how all too often he declared, "There is no God." Nick would simply dismiss my logic and come back with, "It's not a question of God or religion. It's a matter of what's right, and being homosexual is wrong!"

We fought, made up and fought again. But all our arguments solved nothing, and after trying to make it work for five years, I was the one to break the union.

Now I was feeling lonely and displaced at not having my lover by my side. I was also beset by feelings of guilt. Nick had been extremely distraught by our split-up and his despondency at being rejected still burdened me.

"Who is La Glenda and her Super Stars? Are Diana Ross, Bette Midler and Aretha Franklin, and Judy Garland, who is already dead, going to be here?" I joked as we walked into the dimly lit nightclub. The interior was about 25 feet wide and 40 feet long. There were simple white plastic folding chairs and wooden benches. Small tables covered with bright red plastic tablecloths and trimmed with Christmas decorations, surrounded a circular space which was reserved for the dance floor and the stage. Posters of Santa Claus, Xmas trees and snow scenes were tacked up and displayed along the walls.

"What kind of show are we seeing in this motley joint, anyway?" I quipped.

"Oh, I forgot to tell you it's *las locas!* Female impersonators, you know, transvestites. It'll be a hoot! Samuel and Ivan said it's a terrific show. Apparently they only do one performance during the Christmas season. These *locas* are known around the small towns as terrific entertainers. So, it's quite a big deal for the folks around here that they've chosen this barrio for their extravaganza."

Brenda sighed impatiently when she saw the look of disappointment cross my face. Watching a bunch of drag queens was not my idea of authentic native entertainment.

"Come on, Ana, it's better than staying home and watching another movie video."

I relaxed because she was right. Besides, I was weary of vegetating and bored with obsessing over my emotional anguish.

As Brenda and I went to pay for our tickets, two men, one dressed in a custom-made white linen suit and the other wearing an elegant traditional *guayabera* shirt, rushed over to us.

"Your money's no good tonight, ladies," said Ivan, the man in the *guayabera*. He was tall and lean with light brown skin and tight curly chestnut-colored hair. The other man, Samuel, had an olive complexion and very straight black hair that was receding along his forehead. He was of medium height and had a broad muscular build. Both men were quite attractive. We were led to a front row table that had been reserved just for us. Ivan and Samuel immediately ordered drinks. I sipped my cold beer, enjoying the sharp taste. They were each polite and attentive. But as we were all making small talk, I noticed that Brenda preferred Ivan. I wasn't interested in either one.

I looked around. Most of the audience was made up of *campesinos,* poor peasants, although there was also a sprinkling of prosperous country folk. I also noticed that people of all ages, from old men and women to teenagers as young as fourteen, had come to be entertained. The majority of men wore jeans or work pants and cotton shirts with gaudy ties, or tee shirts. Most of the women donned simple skirts and blouses, or dresses that were either home-sewn or purchased at a local general store. But everyone was well-groomed and wore their very best garments for this special evening. By contrast, Brenda and I, in our New York clothing and jewelry, as well as Samuel in his expensive well-tailored suit and Ivan in his extravagant guayabera, looked affluent and out of place.

"This area is called *Bosque de Neblina,* because we're in the highlands and the region has an abundance of mist and light rain." Samuel continued to explain that this was his hometown. His father owned a large farm cultivating a special blend of coffee and an assortment of produce. Although he was from another town, Ivan's family also operated a prosperous hardware concern in the region.

Every few minutes a poor peasant or two approached Samuel and exchanged a few words with obsequious deference. Invariably, they bowed politely as they departed. Samuel responded in a friendly, affable way, but appeared uncomfortable by their fawning. I could see that he was not a snob and immediately liked him for that. His attitude also made me ease up so that I felt less conspicuous and somewhat sheltered by his presence.

The disc jockey played mostly *merengues,* and once in a while a *bolero* or a salsa number. Brenda danced with Ivan and it soon became clear that I was going to be paired off with Samuel. Samuel seemed personable enough and was a smooth dancer. Soon, Nick and my apprehensions faded, and I found myself having a good time.

When the music stopped, the disc jockey made several announcements dealing with local activities and events. Then he presented Samuel, who took the microphone and in turn introduced us. "Dr. Brenda Nieves is a professor of Sociology at New York University, and *la dama* Ana Belmondo is an accomplished advertising executive. These beautiful Puerto Rican sisters live in New York City. Let's welcome them both to our beloved Quisqueya." Brenda and I stood and bowed appreciatively as we received a hearty round of applause.

The lights dimmed and a bright spotlight focused on La Glenda who had on an enormous blonde afro wig and wore a skin-tight flower-print sequined polyester pantsuit. He stood with his muscular arms raised high in the air. Slowly, he brought his hands down, caressing his body, then he shook his shoulders, turned, and spun on his high, spiked heels. Glenda snapped his fingers, and on the fourth count a loud medley of Motown numbers blasted from the loudspeakers. Everyone applauded and El Show began.

Tonight's gala show, La Glenda announced, was going to be devoted to great singing legends of the United States, performed by his *Super Estrellas*. There were five in all, including Glenda. Glenda introduced each one and they sashayed around the stage, glittering under heavy makeup. Pointing with histrionic gestures to their chests, the superstars began to proudly display their array of garish costumes.

Belinda stood about 5 feet 4 inches with a petite build and wore his own natural long black straight hair in a flowing ponytail. Carioca was medium height, portly with a dark brown complexion, and wore a bright orange wig styled into a bob. Altagracia had natural curly blond shoulder-length hair, fair pink skin and a thick muscular body. The last one, Wanda, was very tall with a gaunt body, a sickly pale complexion and a long angular face. His demeanor had an air of melancholy that reminded me of someone, although at that moment I could not think of who it might be.

I had seen transvestites perform in the elegant clubs and funky dives of New York City in places like Greenwich Village and the West forties in Manhattan. But never before had I seen such a ragtag chorus. These costumes were made up of cheap synthetic fabrics, badly cut and sewn. Except for Glenda, who was wearing huge falsies, and Belinda, who appeared to be taking hormone injections and showed some cleavage, their chests were as flat as boards. The heels on most of their shoes were crooked and worn down, in urgent need of repair. Their stockings clearly showed mended patches where slits were now reappearing. All, except for Wanda, had applied makeup with such a variety of glaring colors that they could almost appear as clowns.

But it was Wanda, with his face encased in rice powder with purple rouge and matching lipstick, that looked the most pathetic. His long-sleeved black floor-length gown, dotted with lavender rosettes, hung limply and was exceedingly unflattering. Tall, gawky and with hardly a trace of feminine features, Wanda had to be the ugliest transvestite I had ever seen.

I couldn't imagine how any audience could see these five and not laugh. Yet as I glanced around, everyone was engrossed in the performance.

Glenda did a perfect impersonation of Celia Cruz, who she sang in Spanish, while everyone joined the chorus and clapped in rhythm. That was followed by a quick change into a black bouffant wig and resulted in three Diana Ross numbers.

Then Carioca continued with his rendition of Aretha Franklin, imitating all of her gestures and faultlessly mouthing "Chain of Fools," followed by "Respect" and several other numbers. The crowd went wild when Belinda parodied Cher, and for his finale, stripped off his skirt, exposing his buttocks and a G-string.

Exactly as was done in any other club, during a number customers stepped up and placed money in the performer's waist, collar, chest or wherever else they could manage. If you were giving out big bills, in this case more than five American dollars, you could place the money inside the entertainer's crotch. Belinda kept stuffing bills inside his G-string until it bulged out between his legs.

I was genuinely surprised with the long line of people queuing up to deposit their pesos onto the transvestites. Everyone, women, men, young and old, waited for their chance with exhilaration. Their faces lit up with smiles of delight when they finally got to touch the performers.

Samuel must have seen my astonishment because he tapped my arm gently and whispered, "Many of these people don't even have electricity where they live, Ana. Most are illiterate. They have no TV, no stereos, no cd's, and some have never even seen a movie. They don't understand English and probably may have only heard this music on their portable radios. These *campesinos* come from all around this mountainous territory and look forward to this diversion. They have been saving their pesos for weeks, maybe even months, just to be here tonight. For them it's all a great dazzling spectacle. Can you understand that?"

"Yes." And it was so. All around me folks were gazing at each transvestite in awe, star- struck by all the magnetism and wizardry that was being created just for them. Enchanted, everyone reached out, captivated by all of the glamour that surrounded them.

After an exuberant rendition of Bette Midler singing a combination of World War II songs performed by Altagracia, it was Wanda's turn. Wanda's prominent features covered by the white rice powder and his sad expression made him look like a despondent mime.

A short musical mélange of Judy Garland tunes sounded, and with the first song, *You Made Me Love You,* Wanda opened his sad mouth and stretched his purple lips exquisitely in sync with the words. As he sang, I felt once again that I knew this person. Somewhere in the past I had known Wanda.

❖❖❖

Then it all began to materialize in my mind and it was like gazing at the past through a crystal ball. I recalled the first time I had encountered Utopia, an effeminate man who actually fancied himself to be a female. I was only twelve then and had just gotten my period. My strict Puerto Rican Catholic upbringing did not permit discussions about sex and menstruation. However, my mother had managed after I queried her at age ten to verify that someday, once a month like clockwork, I was indeed going to bleed through my vagina from way inside my body.

"Every single month?" I asked, repeating what my girlfriends had told me, then added, "And there's nothing I can do to stop it?"

That was when my mother told me that the bleeding was perfectly natural.

"Menstruation will make you a woman, Ana, and you'll be ready to bear children. That's when your life will change and your childhood leaves you. No more little girl. You'll become a *señorita,* a virgin. That's also when we all must be very careful to keep a watchful eye on you to make sure the boys keep their distance."

When I insisted on knowing why it was women who had to bleed and not men, my mother told me it was because females were the stronger sex.

"Men are too weak, they could never stand the pain. That's why nature made it so males can't have babies. Besides, it's healthy for us women to discharge all of our impure blood once a month. That makes our insides nice and clean."

None of this made much sense to me, but I also knew that my mother was not going to tell me any more. The rest of my sexual education would have to be gotten from my playmates in the street, or if I was lucky, from the hygiene course at school.

Yet as reticent as my mother was to speak to me of such things as sex and body changes, she welcomed all sorts of visitors into our home. They came in different nationalities and races, single, married, eccentric, straight and gay.

There was Mr. O'Shaugnesey, the elderly Irish man abandoned by his sons and who lived alone. He claimed to communicate with space aliens from Mars and would visit us regularly to confide in my mother about his latest assignments. Mr. O'Shaughnesy would point toward heaven then write on the pad attached to his clipboard, "I'm very busy today reporting to my superiors about who is going on the list to be abducted by the space rays for secret research. But you don't have to worry, Doña Lourdes. I'll never give your name." He'd whisper conspiratorially, "In fact, if danger comes I'll warn you. But not the others... shhh."

Mrs. Watkins, a black woman originally from Georgia, lived with nine cats and fed the strays as well. She'd give them names like Misery, Destiny, Hopeful and Watchful. Mrs. Watkins would come by almost daily at the end of a day, carrying a large pail into which my mother would donate the day's leftovers.

In this way my mother was quite a broad-minded and compassionate person.

Another such visitor was a man in his middle thirties who had renamed himself Utopia. He worked as a manicurist at a beauty salon in Manhattan on West 14th Street. Utopia was tall and ungainly, wore his dark curly hair just above his shoulders, doused his face with rice powder, applied round pink rouge spots on his cheeks and colored his lips bright orange. Utopia's long fingernails were always neatly manicured and painted a dark red. Despite all of this, he always wore the same conservative clothes. He dressed in a plain black shirt and trousers and black shoes. The contrast between Utopia's strange makeup and his austere clothing was startling.

My family lived in the South Bronx back then, through to the end of the 1950's, right off Longwood Avenue and Southern Boulevard. Utopia would come by about two afternoons a week and sit in our kitchen while my mother busied herself preparing the evening's meal. Once a month Utopia complained that he was having menstrual cramps.

"It's that time of the month for me," he'd mutter, and search in his small canvas carrying case. "I've forgotten my Midol tablets again, Doña Lourdes. You couldn't spare a couple, could you?" Whereupon my mom would be quite sympathetic and give him two Midols, or Empirin Compound, depending on what she had in the house. It struck me as odd because Utopia never ever brought his own supply of tablets. We couldn't say he wasn't generous, because he'd always bring us a gift, a box of cookies or a cake from our local bakery. Sometimes he'd have a small present for me, a box of sachet, toilet water or a bottle of nail polish.

When I asked my mom how come Utopia could have cramps, she told me that they were actually not the sort of cramps she and I got.

"The pain's mostly in his head because he doesn't have a uterus," she'd say. "But, Utopia feels the ache, same as we do. So, what's the harm in giving him a couple of pills? And it makes him feel better, same as us."

More than once I persisted in questioning my mother to explain just why Utopia thought he was a woman when he was in fact a man. She always responded in her usual no-nonsense logic that some people were simply born that way.

"God doesn't always do a perfect job, although I'm sure He tries. But Utopia is one of God's creatures, just like everybody else."

A few of our neighbors didn't approve of Utopia visiting us and said so. Doña Josefina, who lived on the second floor, was the worst gossip and had the most to say. "He's not a good example for a young girl, especially a *señorita* like Ana. What kind of person is that... a man who paints himself and thinks he's a woman?"

"It's better than a man who considers himself a lover and then goes after my little girl!" my mother would snap back. "Utopia doesn't bother anyone. He's not vulgar or dishonest, doesn't gossip. People like that are always welcome in my home!"

Utopia wasn't his original name. Once he revealed to us that he had been baptized Francisco Luis. One day when my mother wasn't around (since she would have considered my question rude behavior), I got up the nerve to ask why he had renamed himself Utopia.

"*Ay,* Ana, *mi hijita,* let me tell you my story. You already know I've been a widow for seven years." Then he pointed to the gold wedding band on his ring finger, left hand. "That's why I always wear black. Carlos and I were married only three short years. But to me they represent a lifetime of happiness. He brought me out, you see. Carlos did. Even as a child I knew I was meant to be a woman. I never played with my older brother, who was five years my senior, because I hated boy games. I was always with my twin sisters, who were only a couple of years older than me. At home they used to tie ribbons in my hair and I loved it.

"Why, by the age of four, I was already sewing the most beautiful dresses, hats and elegant clothes for my sisters' dolls. I would use scraps of material, old buttons and snaps, or just about anything I could find. My sisters' dolls were the envy of our neighborhood. But when I started school at age six, my mother abruptly stopped me. One day I came home and found that my wooden sewing box was gone.

"Inside was my collection of sewing needles, wonderful colored spools of thread, sequins, gorgeous buttons and lovely pieces of lace and material. All that I had gathered with great care and love during my entire young life had been discarded. My universe was in that wooden box. Can you imagine? I felt horrible. But when I complained, my mother took my father's large leather strap and gave me a violent beating, shouting with each whip of the strap. 'You're not a girl! God damn it, you have a penis. A penis! You are a boy... not a girl!'

"Next day I developed a high fever and had to be kept home from school. Yet my mother promised that if she ever caught me wearing ribbons or sewing for dolls again, she'd whip me some more. Only next time I might not survive. She would not live with the shame of having a *maricón*, a faggot, for a son.

"My mother told me they preferred me dead rather than queer. I withdrew after that and pretended to be the kind of son they wanted. Later on I made believe that I lusted after women. This pleased my parents and my family. But I never felt any passion for women. I tried, but never got beyond a friendly kiss.

"Then at age 24, after my studies in Havana, I emigrated from Cuba to go to graduate school in New York City. It was at Fordham University where I met my Carlos. I was working on a masters degree in Early Education, which by the way I never did finish. Although my Carlos wasn't a student, you know. No. He worked as a porter at the school, cleaning up. Uneducated he was, never went beyond the sixth grade. But he knew what love was, my beautiful young man, a Chicano *campesino,* from Texas with a soul as generous as the heavens. He brought me out, you see. After loving Carlos, there was no denying who I was. Oh, he was so wonderful, Ana! He was my one and only. I've not fallen in love since he passed away. I'm sorry you and Doña Lourdes never met him."

Utopia paused, pulled out his wallet and showed me a picture of Carlos.

"Isn't he the handsomest man you ever saw? Look at those dark gentle eyes."

Utopia paused, trying to hold back tears.

"We got married, not legally of course, because the law wouldn't allow it. But we wrote our own vows and a friend, who's a wonderful spiritualist and healer, performed the ceremony. Carlos renamed me Utopia, because he said that in me he had found a perfect world."

After that, Francisco Luis had legally changed his name to Utopia Echevarría, also adopting Carlos' surname. Sadly, after three blissful years together, recounted Utopia, Carlos took ill and died of a ruptured appendix. Apparently, he was very frightened of doctors and hospitals and waited too long to be treated.

I remember trying to understand why Utopia preferred to be a woman. I thought about my three older brothers, my stepfather, uncles, and of all the power and freedom they possessed. When boys had lots of girlfriends, or men seduced women, they were called *macho* and virile. Males were sanctioned as the conquistadors of the females. But as females, if we went out with more than one boy, we were automatically labeled *putitas,* little whores.

Men didn't have to bleed, or get cramps or be afraid of getting pregnant. I had heard about the danger and anguish of childbearing... who and why would anybody want such pain? Also, I could not understand what was so wonderful about making dolls' clothes. I hated sewing and had never cared much for dolls, preferring stuffed animals. Ultimately, I never did make any sense out of Utopia's obsession, since there seemed to be no power, no tangible gain or obvious pleasure in his desire to be female, only distress and precious little freedom in this man's world.

❖ ❖ ❖

Samuel's whisper inquiring if I wanted a drink brought me back to La Casita Disco Club. I requested another beer. Wanda was still singing with his long arms, large hands and bony fingers outstretched, lamenting "Oh, my man, I love him so... and I'll never let him go" Judy Garland's voice echoed out to a mute and mesmerized audience. At the finish a thunderous applause sounded and men as well as women wiped tears from their eyes.

"What a sad creature that was," said Brenda, noticeably moved. I wanted to tell her about Utopia and his resemblance to Wanda. But as soon as El Show was over, the disc jockey began blasting away with a wild and quick *merengue,* and no one would have heard me. Samuel took my hand and we followed the crowd right out onto the dance floor.

As we were dancing I saw that all of the transvestites had refreshed their makeup, made a few slight changes in their outfits and had reappeared. They stood lined up at the bar like chorus girls, giggling, swaying their hips to the music, and glancing coquettishly at the men who watched them. Although it is accepted that two women may dance jointly, it is the custom here that two men never dance as a couple.

I became intrigued. Would these *campesinos* with a macho tradition ask other men, dressed as women, to dance? I wondered. When our dance finished I told Samuel that I was too tired to go on and preferred to sit for a few moments. A bit disappointed, Samuel excused himself and said he had to talk to a few folks, but that he'd return in a little while. Nothing could suit me better. It was my way of being able to observe what might unfold.

From my ringside table I had a full view of Glenda, Belinda, Carioca, Altagracia and Wanda as they sipped their drinks, joked teasingly and flirted openly with the bartenders and onlookers. "I've never seen such gorgeous muscles all gathered in one place," said Belinda in a loud sing-song voice. "Do you think we can touch it, handsome? Your muscle, I mean," joked Altagracia, winking at the man who had been staring at them. Their vitality and joyous note was so compelling that immediately folks came up to the bar and bought them drinks.

A handsome *campesino* with a red scarf tied round his neck was the first to ask Belinda to dance. Belinda threw back his mane of long black hair, took a hanky from his cleavage and delicately dabbed his forehead, then with a sweet smile nodded and accepted his invitation. Then, as another *campesino* approached Carioca, he playfully felt the man's biceps, rolled his eyes and shouted, "You're so big and hard... I don't dare say no!" In a matter of minutes, Altagracia and Glenda were also out on the dance floor laughing with their male partners and swaying their hips to the percussive sounds of a rapid salsa number by Ray Barretto and his orchestra.

A moment later, another man with a nervous expression came up to Wanda and managed an awkward bow. Wanda smiled demurely and slowly placed his hands on the man's shoulders. As he clasped Wanda tightly, they gyrated together in perfect harmony to the music. Each one of the transvestites radiated a festive energy that saturated the crowd with merriment.

Even the women came up to them and smiled with admiration. New partners cut in while they danced, demanding their turn with the "ladies." The transvestites' elation at being perceived and accepted as females became irresistible. I, too, had become convinced they were women and whispered, "Look at those beaming ladies," forgetting that these were men masquerading as females. I no longer saw their pitiful costumes, worn-down foot gear or bizarre makeup, for now I, too, was spellbound.

In expressing their feminine energies so outlandishly, the transvestites were able to share their personal euphoria with all of us. And, once again I remembered the last time I had seen Utopia. After having visited us steadily for a year, Utopia disappeared for about six months. Then one day he telephoned and announced he had remarried and wanted us to meet his new husband.

Utopia arrived with Freddy, a shy man in his late forties who was divorced and the father of three children. I had never seen Utopia looking so blissful and content before. Although Utopia's makeup remained the same, his clothes were quite cheerful. It was early July, and he wore a bright blue silk shirt, white cotton vest and pants, and a pair of white patent-leather boots with tassels. The couple proudly showed us their wedding bands. Utopia announced that he and Freddy were moving to Los Angeles, California, to make a new start. He wept when he said good-bye.

"Doña Lourdes, you've been like a mother to me, and Ana has been my little sister. I'll miss you both very much. You're the best girlfriends a woman can have. We must write to each other."

He gave my mother a bottle of perfume and presented me with an expensive leather-bound nail and cuticle care set. During the next couple of years we did receive a few postcards and a letter or two, always saying how happy he and Freddy were. My

mom was not much for writing, and I was not interested in communicating with older folks of any kind.
In time we lost touch with Utopia.

This evening as I watched Wanda with his purple
lips curving into a wide smile, I so clearly recalled
Utopia as he had appeared during his last visit,
ecstatically happy and in love.

I sat at La Casita Disco Club and like everyone
else there was delighted to be included in this fantasy.
Suddenly, I found myself grateful for such a splendid
illusion. It seemed to me an unpretentious act of generosity on the part of these performers.

When Samuel returned, he asked if I was ready
to dance. With a feeling of absolute confidence, just
like the *super estrellas,* I put my arms around
Samuel and we spun out on the dance floor. I twirled,
stepped and shook all the sorrow out of my being.
When Brenda passed by, I tried my best to share my
feelings and yelled in her direction, "For these 'ladies'
it's not about pain, anguish or suffering. It's about a
woman's power to give joy, to enchant others." But
the La Casita Disco Club was pulsating with the
sounds of a rapid *merengue* and Brenda motioned
that she couldn't hear.

"Never mind." I waved. Before I left for New York
City, I would find the right moment in which to share
with Brenda how I had learned to appreciate my own
joyous energy during a celebration of the female spirit, on the night when I remembered Utopia and
bonded with the "ladies" of GLENDA Y SU SUPER
ESTRELLAS.